"You're way too easy to talk to."

"Yeah, I get that a lot. It must be the overalls."

The sound of his own laughter surprised him. Scott marveled at how quickly she'd found a way to make him *want* to laugh again. "Must be. Well, that, and you ask a lotta questions."

"Creative people are curious by nature," Jenna informed him. "It comes with the territory when you hang out with me."

Translation: *This is who I am—take it or leave it.* He admired her sassy attitude more than he could say. "Thanks for the warning. Ready for a refill?"

"Actually, what I'd really like is to see the chapel." She tilted her head. "Do you have time to show it to me?"

He couldn't think of anything he'd like half as much as spending some more time with the perky artist. "It's in pretty rough shape, so I'm afraid there's not much to see."

"Sometimes things aren't as bad as they seem on first glance." Meeting his eyes with her direct, unflinching gaze, she smiled. "I prefer to see for myself and make up my own mind."

He sensed she was referring to more than decrepit old buildings.

Mia Ross loves great stories. She enjoys reading about fascinating people, long-ago times and exotic places. But only for a little while, because her reality is pretty sweet. Married to her college sweetheart, she's the proud mom of two amazing kids, whose schedules keep her hopping. Busy as she is, she can't imagine trading her life for anyone else's—and she has a pretty good imagination. You can visit her online at miaross.com.

Books by Mia Ross

Love Inspired

Barrett's Mill Series

Blue Ridge Reunion
Sugar Plum Season
Finding His Way Home ✓

Holiday Harbor Series

Rocky Coast Romance
Jingle Bell Romance
Seaside Romance

Hometown Family
Circle of Family
A Gift of Family
A Place for Family

Visit the Author Profile page at Harlequin.com
for more titles.

Finding His Way Home

Mia Ross

HARLEQUIN® LOVE INSPIRED®

Recycling programs
for this product may
not exist in your area.

LOVE INSPIRED BOOKS

ISBN-13: 978-0-373-04329-3

Finding His Way Home

www.Harlequin.com

Printed in U.S.A.

Faith is being sure of what we hope for
and certain of what we do not see.
—*Hebrews* 11:1

For brave souls everywhere
making the most of their second chances.

Acknowledgments

To the very talented folks who help me
make my books everything they can be:
Elaine Spencer, Melissa Endlich and the
dedicated staff at Love Inspired.

More thanks to the gang at Seekerville
(seekerville.net). It's a great place
to hang out with readers—and writers!

I've been blessed with a wonderful network of
supportive and encouraging family and friends.
You inspire me every day!

Chapter One

*William Henry Barrett. Cherished on earth
and in heaven.*

Hands folded in front of him, Scott Barrett stared down at the granite headstone that marked his grandfather's resting place in the Barrett's Mill Cemetery. Solid and straightforward, in Scott's mind the stone and its message couldn't have summed up Granddad any better. A kind, hardworking man all his life, Will had given everything he had to his family and the sleepy Virginia town that bore their name.

And now he was gone.

Out of necessity, over the years Scott had learned to mask his emotions behind a cool facade that gave nothing away. But now, facing up to the consequences of bad choices he'd made long ago, a wave of remorse threatened to overwhelm him. If only he'd taken the high road, he lamented silently, he would've been able to get here in time to say goodbye.

Unfortunately, some mistakes took root in your life like weeds and spoiled what might have been a good thing if you'd tended to it properly from the start. That lesson, among many others, had been drummed into his head every day for the past three years. From his childhood through graduation day, his mother had complained to him and his four brothers that Barrett men never learned anything the easy way. And he was Barrett to the core.

Granddad had accepted that, Scott recalled as he sat down on the freshly turned ground in front of the stone. He'd seen all that in his headstrong grandson, and more.

I'm sad to see you go, he'd said the last time Scott left their tiny hometown in the Blue Ridge Mountains for some vague destination. *But I'll be here waiting for you when you get back.*

Leaning his head against the marker, Scott followed his memories back in time and dredged up a visual of Granddad, smiling and waving as he drove away. Closing his eyes, he swallowed hard around the sudden lump in his throat. "I'm sorry I missed out on seeing you again, Granddad. I got home as fast as I could."

The warm spring breeze ruffled through his hair, and he felt a small measure of calm settle over him. Even though he knew it was unlikely, he chose to believe it was his grandfather reaching down from heaven to let him know he understood.

"Scott?"

An unfamiliar voice jolted him from his

brooding, and he looked up to find a stranger looking down at him. A very pretty stranger, he noted with surprise. Dressed in a pink tank top and faded overalls spattered with every color imaginable, she had dark, curly hair and eyes that made him think of a flawless summer sky. She was holding a spade and a bushel basket filled with flowers, and she set them next to Granddad's grave as if she meant to stay.

In the interest of avoiding trouble, he'd developed a habit of ducking his head and avoiding eye contact whenever possible. But this was another place, he reminded himself, and here that kind of behavior would come across as rude. Recalling the manners his mother had insisted they all learn and use, he got to his feet and did his best to put on a friendly face. "That's me. I've been gone awhile, so I don't think we've met."

"Jenna Reed," she replied, offering a slender hand covered in flecks of purple and green. "I moved here last summer and started up Reed's Artworks. You may have seen my sign out on the highway on your way into town."

That explained her unusual clothes, and he tried to sound friendly. "I did, actually. How's business?"

"Oh, you know how it is," she said breezily, as if thcy'd known each other for months instead of mere seconds. "Up and down, depending on the day."

Like his life, Scott added silently. Meeting this lovely, outgoing woman in a cemetery had to qualify as an up, though. Maybe it was a sign of better things to come. "Yeah, I hear you. How'd you know who I was?"

"I've gotten to know your family since I've been here, and I recognized you from the picture of you and your brothers on your grandmother's mantel."

"How's she doing?" When he realized he'd just admitted he hadn't gone to visit her yet, he mentally cringed. Acting without thinking had gotten him in a world of trouble, he cautioned himself. Now that he'd escaped the worst of it, he really needed to work on being less impulsive.

"You know Olivia. Everything's fine, even when the rest of us think it's falling apart. At the end, she was the most positive one in your whole family. I've never seen anyone so strong."

"Yup, that's Gram."

The conversation stalled right there, and he searched for a way to grind his rusty social skills back into gear. Then he remembered the shovel and flowers and nodded toward them. "Whatcha got there?"

It wasn't smooth, but judging by her quick smile, she either didn't notice his floundering or didn't mind. "Flowers for Will from the Crossroads Church. We thought he should have them year-round, so I volunteered to plant some perennials that will come up every spring."

"That's nice of you." He couldn't imagine why she'd do such a thing for someone she wasn't related to. In the world he'd been living in, it was everyone for himself, and people didn't help anyone else unless there was something in it for them. And then, out of nowhere, he heard himself ask, "Want a hand?"

"Sure, thanks."

He couldn't believe what he'd just done, but there was no way he could change his mind without looking like a total jerk. It wasn't as if he had anything pressing to do this morning, so he picked up the shovel and got to work turning the soil back for a small garden.

"Let's make an arch," she suggested, pointing in a semicircle. "That will look nicer, don't you think?"

It didn't matter much to him, since he thought the flowers were more than enough, but he appreciated her asking for his input. It had been a long time since he'd been treated with the kind of respect this perky stranger was showing him. "Sounds good."

"Your grandmother has the prettiest gardens," Jenna commented while she set peat pots of various flowers into a pattern that seemed to make sense to her. Apparently not satisfied, she rearranged them several times until she finally quit and sat back on the heels of her sneakers. "What do you think?"

"Pretty."

Angling a look up at him, she gave him a teasing smile. "The flowers or me?"

He caught himself smiling back, and alarms started clanging in his head. Another hard-won lesson had taught him that women were nothing but trouble, and pretty ones were the worst of all. He had a feeling the worst of all were the artistic kind with freckles sprinkled across their noses.

Being drawn to her so quickly baffled—and worried—him, and he firmly put his conflicting reactions to her aside as he got back to his digging. She didn't say anything, but he could feel her watching him, studying him like some new species she'd discovered under a microscope. His movements allowed him to glance over at her every shovelful or so, and at one point he met those amazing eyes head-on.

Setting down the pot she was holding, she gave him a gentle smile. "Did you want to ask me something?"

A lot of somethings, he thought, but one zoomed to the top of his list. He plunged the shovel into the ground and leaned on the battered red handle. "How much do you know about me?"

"More than you'd like, I'm guessing." Another smile, this one tinged with compassion. "We all make mistakes, Scott."

"Most folks don't make the kind that land them in prison."

"I try not to judge people based on what they might have done before, but on what I see in them right now." Pausing, she gave him an assessing look. "I see a guy who was in the wrong place at the wrong time with the wrong crowd. He owned up to his part in what they did and took his punishment for it. Now he's come back to his hometown, where people care about him, hoping to put his life back together. How'm I doing?"

Those warnings in his mind blared again, but quieter this time. Despite his misgivings, Scott allowed himself a slight grin. "Fine. Makes me wonder how someone as young as you would come by that opinion, though."

"Just how young do you think I am?"

He wasn't touching that one, so he said, "Well, I'm twenty-seven, and I'm thinking you're a couple years younger than that. How'm I doing?" he added, echoing her earlier question.

"Fine," she parroted him with a little smirk, then got serious. "You're not the only person in the world who's had to shake off their past and start over again, y'know."

With that, she took a trowel from her basket and began digging in the earth he'd turned. It struck him as an odd thing to say, but she didn't volunteer anything more. Taking her silence as a hint that she was done discussing that topic, he began shaping the crescent she'd requested. "So how do you like it here?"

"It's a charming little town, and the people arc really nice."

He'd known enough women to hear a qualifier in there somewhere, and he nudged. "But?"

After hesitating for a few moments, she sighed. "I've been here almost a year. The summer art fairs will be starting up soon, and I'll be on my way."

Her tone had a tinge of resignation in it, and he frowned. He'd just met her, but the thought of this cheerful painter being unhappy bothered him for some reason. "You don't sound thrilled with that."

"It's the way it is," she replied with a shrug. "I've learned that things go better for me if I'm not in one place too long."

Scott understood that philosophy all too well. It had governed his life for years, and at first it had been fun. The excitement of drifting around the country, working at this job or that one, following the good weather, had given him some great memories. Then, one steamy Houston afternoon, the thing he valued most had been wrenched away from him.

That fateful day, he'd lost his freedom. It had taken him a long time to get it back, and he'd die before he would let anyone take it from him again.

Jenna knew a mess when she saw one.

Wearing tattered jeans and a well-loved rock-concert T-shirt that hung loosely on his tall frame, Scott Barrett definitely fit the bill. While they worked, she noticed he was careful to keep his distance from her. She'd never been to prison herself, but it wasn't hard to imagine why he'd become so guarded about his personal space. There was something about him that spoke to her, though, and it was more than the slightly shaggy brown hair and determined set of his jaw. When he glanced over at her, she finally pegged what had snared her attention.

His eyes. Dark and wary, they connected with hers for a moment before flitting away. It was as if he didn't want her to catch him observing her. She did a lot of portrait work for clients, and it had made her adept at reading people. Her instincts told her he wasn't eyeing her in a creepy, stalkerish kind of way. Because she moved around so much, she knew how it felt to be an outsider in a community, but for him it was different. He should have felt at home here in the place where he'd grown up, but he didn't. Knowing that made her feel sad for him, and she hunted for a way to ease his mind.

Hoping to draw him out a little, she attempted to resuscitate their lapsed conversation. "So, it must be nice to be back in your hometown."

"Didn't have anywhere else to go," he muttered, stabbing at fresh ground with the spade.

He was digging outside the area she'd shown him for Will's garden, but out of respect for his current attitude she chose not to point that out. Instead, she tried again. "I've lived in lots of different places myself. I think Denver was my favorite with the mountains and so many interesting spots to paint. How 'bout you?"

"I liked Texas. Till they told me I couldn't leave," he added with a wry grin.

The dark gallows humor caught her by surprise, and she couldn't help laughing. "I can't believe you can joke about that."

"You give a man enough time alone with his thoughts, one of two things happens—he either goes crazy or he comes to terms with what happened. I'm not the loony-bin type."

"I'm glad," she said reflexively, getting a

questioning look in reply. "I mean, for your family. They've all missed you so much."

"I missed them, too." Staring at his grandfather's marker, he sighed. "More than you could possibly know."

He had the same rangy, muscular build as his brothers, but there was something different about him she couldn't quite identify. An artist as much by nature as profession, she'd always been inquisitive about everything and everyone around her. What made them unique, what made them tick. While she recognized that Scott was an individual with his own qualities, she couldn't help comparing him to the Barretts she'd gotten to know. There was no denying he had his own vibe, and she searched for a way to define it.

Out of nowhere, it hit her: he was wounded. Judging by his pragmatic way of looking at life, it wasn't from being locked up, at least not entirely. Since they'd just met, she didn't want to pry into what was certainly very personal business, so she tamped down her curiosity and turned her attention to the cluster of forget-me-nots she was planting.

They didn't talk at all, but he seemed to understand where she needed the soil dug out and stayed a few shovelfuls ahead of her while she worked. When she'd planted the last of the flowers, she stood and wiped the dirt off her palms onto her overalls. Holding out a hand, she smiled. "Thanks for the help, Scott. It was great to meet you, but I should be getting back to my studio."

After hesitating for a moment, he gently took her hand, shaking it as if it was made of glass. Those dark eyes connected directly with hers for the first time, and as hard as she tried, she couldn't make herself look away. There was that pain again, but now it was joined by the hopeful look of a lonely little boy who thought maybe—just maybe—he'd found a new friend.

While she knew it would be completely insane for her to get involved with this guy, she couldn't shake the feeling that he needed her. With every instinct screaming for her to back away and leave him be, she heard herself say, "All this digging sure is thirsty work. Can I buy you a glass of iced tea at The Whistlestop?"

At first, he didn't react at all. Then, slowly, as if something that had been frozen was thawing a bit, a slow grin worked its way across his chiseled features. "You're not from the South, are you?"

"Chicago. Why?"

"Around here, we call it sweet tea. And you don't have to buy me any, 'cause I've got a gallon jug of Mom's at the house. No one makes it any better."

A quick glance around showed her nothing but trees and gravestones. "I don't see a car or a house for that matter. How far did you walk to get here?"

"Over that hill," he replied, pointing to a modest rise that led into the nearby woods. When she hesitated, he frowned. "Unless you'd rather not be alone out in the boonies with a guy you just met. I'd totally understand."

"It's not that," she assured him quickly, relieved to see some of the tension leave his face. "It's just that I've been all over the area painting landscapes, and I didn't realize there was a house over this way. It's so overgrown, I figured it was all woods and deer trails."

"It is." Chuckling, he picked up her empty basket and balanced the shovel on his shoulder. "That's what I like most about it."

When he stepped back, she realized he was cueing her to walk in front of him. A Southern gentleman in raggedy jeans and a faded T-shirt, she mused with a little grin. That was the last thing she'd expect to find in this tall, quiet man clearly laboring to steer his life back on track.

Intuition told her there was a lot more to Scott Barrett than his good looks and cool reserve. Peeling away those layers would be fascinating. Or dangerous, that irritating little voice cautioned her while she and Scott walked side by side toward the top of the hill. Harsh experience had taught her that the male species was like that, which was why she resisted getting tangled up with anyone in particular. Her gypsy lifestyle enabled her to stay clear of the doomed cycle she'd watched her hopelessly romantic mother go through over and over like a hamster on a wheel. Always frantically running at top speed, never getting anywhere.

Determined to avoid that sort of endless heartache, Jenna had chosen to live each day as it came. When circumstances allowed, she shared those moments with someone. When that wasn't reasonable, she enjoyed them on her own. As an only child, she'd grown up appreciating her own company, so solitude didn't bother her. To her mind, it was better than throwing everything you had into a relationship only to wind up bitter and lonely in the end.

It was a beautiful day, she chided herself, not the time for serious thoughts. As she and Scott made their way through the sunlit hillside meadow, she took a deep breath of air scented with honeysuckle and the wild roses that rambled alongside the faint path that wound through the tall grass. Spots of color here and there showed her patches of fresh buttercups and lilies of the valley, along with wildflowers that ranged from periwinkle blue to deep, vibrant pink. A hawk soared into view overhead, sailing effortlessly on the warm spring breeze in search of his breakfast.

He spotted something and dived, arcing back into the sky with a small rodent clutched in his claws. Impressed by his hunting display, Jenna watched him until he banked in midair and sped off into the distance with his prize.

"Amazing, huh?" Scott asked in a tone laced with the same respect she'd felt for the hawk. "I've always wondered what they see from up there."

"Us?"

"Yeah, but what does he think of us?" When she gave him a blank look, he went on. "I mean, does he think we're interesting, like we do with him? Or does he think we're nuts, racing around all the time and not accomplishing much of anything?"

"So you're the philosophical type," she teased. "Is there anything else I should know?"

"I don't know. Is there?" Raising an eyebrow, he gave her a mischievous grin that made her laugh.

"Don't you be trying that on me, Barrett. I've met all your brothers, and I've seen enough of that troublemaker smile to know better."

"Busted." Still grinning, he said, "But to answer your question, I guess I was always the thinker in the family. Greg and Connor are the responsible ones, Paul's the jock, Jason's the clown and I'm the serious one."

If that was the case, how on earth had he landed in such a bad situation in Texas? she wondered. She'd never ask him that, of course, but she couldn't help wondering, just the same.

"Her name was Kelly," he said, completely out of the blue. "And yes, I was in love with her, and yes, she used that against me. She asked me to pick her and her brothers up at the bank." Pausing, he grimaced and shook his head. "Unfortunately, she neglected to tell me they'd be coming out carrying a bunch of cash that didn't belong to them. By the time I knew what was happening, we were on the run from the cops."

"With you as the innocent getaway driver." Jenna filled in the blank tersely. "Nice girl."

"Well, not so innocent," he corrected her in a tone devoid of emotion. "I could've climbed outta the car and left them to the cops, but I didn't. I tried to talk them into surrendering, but that went about how you'd expect. By the time the police caught up to us, I was pretty much as guilty as they were. I told the detective I had no idea what they had planned for that bank, but Kelly and her brothers claimed otherwise. It ended up being their word against mine, and there were three of them."

When he stopped talking, Jenna tried to come up with some encouraging words. He'd been through a lot, and she didn't want to make him feel any worse than he already did by saying the wrong thing. "Well, now you're here, at home with your family. You can put all those bad times behind you."

He didn't respond to that, but from his sigh, she knew he wasn't buying her upbeat assessment of his situation. For some reason she didn't begin to understand, she really wanted to prove it to him. The question was, how?

As they crested the hill, that dilemma was blown from her mind as she took in the view down in the shallow valley. She knew she was standing there like some kind of moronic statue, but all she could think of to say was "Wow."

Chapter Two

Although his trek down memory lane hadn't been all that pleasant, Scott was amused by Jenna's awestruck reaction to where he was living. Built in 1866 when the old sawmill was put into service, the original Barrett farmhouse wasn't much to look at these days, with its sagging roof and sad excuse for a front porch. But the timbers holding it all up were solid Virginia oak, and they'd still be standing for many generations to come.

Nearby, in a partially overgrown clearing, a tiny chapel with half a roof was losing its battle against the encroaching trees. He'd hacked some of the worst offenders down, but he had a lot of work ahead of him yet. And that didn't count shoring up the building itself. To most folks, he was certain the place would've looked like a lost cause right out of the gate, but it suited Scott perfectly. It gave him plenty to do, tucked away in the woods with only the wildlife for company. Considering people's varying responses to him since his return, he actually preferred hanging out with the animals.

Angling a look up at him, his pretty guest said, "I wish I'd known about this spot sooner. With all the different colors and shafts of light coming down through the branches, it would make a great painting."

"Most folks've forgotten all about it," he acknowledged.

"How did you end up here, though? You've got family in town and over in Cambridge. Why aren't you staying with one of them?"

Her forthright manner caught him off

guard. He'd grown accustomed to people who kept their mouths shut and their heads down. The few old acquaintances he'd seen since coming back to Barrett's Mill were polite but understandably reserved with him. This slender woman looked him straight in the eye and spoke openly to him. He wasn't sure if that appealed to him or not, but it made her different, that was for sure.

"I like it out here," he replied finally. "It's quiet."

She laughed at that. "This whole town is quiet, but I guess I understand you wanting your privacy. I'm the same way."

He wouldn't have put it quite that way, but since she seemed to accept his explanation, he decided to go along. And since she'd offered something personal about herself, he felt it was only fair to do the same. "Actually, Granddad left me this place in his will. There's three acres here that connect to the back of the sawmill property. There's the house and chapel, with a small trust fund to restore them, and I get to live here as long as I want. It's not a fortune, but I don't need much."

"That sounds like Will," she commented with a fond smile. "Taking care of someone but making sure they have to work for it. He gave you a lifeline but arranged things so you're able to keep your dignity."

What was left of it, anyway, Scott added silently. He wasn't comfortable voicing that thought, so he settled for something a little safer. "Yeah."

She gave him a long, curious look, and he braced himself for what might come out of her mouth next.

"You said something about sweet tea?" she asked as she began walking again.

"Yes, ma'am. Not that way, though," he cautioned before she reached the front porch steps. "All those boards are rotten, and you'll go straight through. I already rebuilt the ones out back, so they're much safer."

"How come you did them first?"

He didn't answer, and when she rounded the corner of the house, she paused with a sigh. "Oh, I see why."

Behind the cottage, Sterling Creek wound its way through centuries-old trees on its way to wherever it was going. Sunlight dappled the water, giving the stream a sparkle to go with its cheerful sound. He wasn't normally big on landscaping and such, but sitting on the rough-hewn stairs and listening to the water brought him the kind of peace that had eluded him for more years than he cared to count. It hadn't escaped him that he'd finally found that calm here in the woods surrounding the hometown he couldn't wait to escape from when he was younger.

"This section of the creek was pretty much clogged up when I got here," Scott explained as he went ahead to open the door he'd cobbled together from scrap wood. It didn't have much style, but it was a big improvement over the old one that had been rotting on the hinges. At least it kept out the bold raccoons that had been trotting in and out as if they owned the place. "I spent a few days clearing it out so the creek would run like it used to when I was a kid."

He cringed at the nostalgic twinge in his voice, but Jenna eased his concern with a smile. "That's really sweet. It sounds like you have great memories of this place."

"Some of my best," he confided, following her inside. Grateful that he'd bothered to wash the dishes this morning, he reached into the small fridge sitting on the counter and brought out a jug of sweet tea. "My brothers and I spent a lot of summer days hanging out at the swimming hole upstream with our friends."

Sitting in one of the two seats he had to offer, Jenna gave him a cute smirk as she took the glass he handed her. "I'm guessing some of those friends were girls in bikinis and cutoff shorts."

"A few," he acknowledged with a grin of his own. "We *were* the Barrett boys, after all."

"I'm well aware of your killer reputation." Taking a sip of her tea, she glanced around the kitchen. "So what are your plans for this room?"

Torn back to the studs, it wasn't much to look at right now, and he appreciated her not mentioning it. "Once I get the framing done, there's some scrap oak at the mill I can use to make bead board like the kind that used to be in here before the termites shredded it. It'll take a while, but I want to keep things as original as I can."

"Because that's how it was when your grandfather grew up here."

That she'd picked up on that detail absolutely floored him, and he stared over at her in disbelief. Apparently, she understood his response because she explained, "When Paul and Jason were rehabbing the mill so they could reopen your family's furniture business, they said that kind of thing a lot. Your brothers put in a ton of work, but they never complained because it was all for Will."

Again, the stab of guilt hit Scott hard, and he did his best to roll with the unwelcome sensation. In an effort to stall long enough to regain his composure, he spun the other chair around to straddle it and faced her across the table. He swallowed some of his tea and rested his arms over the back of the chair, rolling his glass back and forth between his hands.

"I wish I could've been here. Y'know, to say goodbye." When it occurred to him he'd just confessed his deepest pain to a stranger, he growled, "You're way too easy to talk to."

"Yeah, I get that a lot. It must be the overalls."

The sound of his own laughter surprised him. Far from the cynical snort he'd adopted, it had a lighthearted quality that appealed to him. Beyond the pleasant sound of it, he marveled at how quickly she'd found a way to make him *want* to laugh again. It had been a long time since he'd had a reason to do it, and he had to admit it felt good. "Must be. Well, that and you ask a lotta questions."

"Creative people are curious by nature," she informed him with another smirk. "It comes with the territory when you hang out with me."

Translation: this is who I am, take it or leave it. He admired her sassy attitude more than he could say, and he couldn't imagine any grown man with a pulse choosing anything other than to accept this bright, engaging woman just the way she was. "Thanks for the warning. Ready for a refill?"

"Actually, what I'd really like is to see the chapel." She tilted her head in the questioning pose that seemed to be part of her personality. "Do you have time to show it to me?"

He had nothing but time these days, and he couldn't think of anything he'd like half as much as spending some more of it with the perky artist he'd stumbled across in the cemetery. Since it didn't seem wise to tell her that, he set his glass on the table and stood. "It's in pretty rough shape, so I'm afraid there's not much to see."

"Sometimes things aren't as bad as they seem on first glance." Meeting his eyes with her direct, unflinching gaze, she smiled. "I prefer to see for myself and make up my own mind."

He sensed she was referring to more than decrepit old buildings, and an odd sensation fanned through his chest. Since he'd never experienced it before, he wasn't sure what it was or what it meant. As Jenna walked past him, something coaxed him to fall in behind her, eager as an old hound dying for some attention from her.

Pathetic, he admitted with a sigh, but true. The problem was, the last time he'd let a woman lead him around, she'd landed him in the worst mess of his life. That betrayal had taught him that trusting his heart was foolish, at best. So while he might enjoy Jenna's bubbly company, for the sake of his sanity that was as far as he could allow a friendship with her to go.

Logical by nature, he knew his stern resolution to keep things light should have eased his concerns. Instead, he had the sinking feeling that choosing to follow the safe route with Jenna would cost him the chance at something amazing.

Quite simply, the sight of that forgotten church broke Jenna's heart.

Without maintenance, the clapboards had rotted and fallen away in many spots, and those that remained were a pale dried-out gray. It struck her as being the color of surrender, and it had absolutely no business being on God's house. The steps weren't good for anything but kindling, and what was left of the roof looked ready to collapse at the slightest hint of a breeze.

"It's looked better," Scott commented wryly, bracing his hands on either side of the door frame to haul himself up to the gaping front entrance. "I found the front doors, but they're toast. They have a nice arch to them, though, and I'll build new ones to fit after I get the roof squared away."

Offering her a hand, he helped her climb up into the entryway. Once inside the single room, she stood there for a few moments to let her eyes take it all in. She'd anticipated a complete disaster and was pleasantly surprised to see that while it was in deplorable condition, the small church had been swept clean of debris. Here and there, she noticed a fresh beam or piece of lumber shoring up the weaker sections.

Some people might have considered them a futile attempt to halt the decay, but to her eyes they looked hopeful. The way Scott did right now, she added with a little smile.

She got the feeling he wanted her to approve of what he'd accomplished so far, and she was more than happy to oblige him. "You've been busy in here. I can already imagine how it'll look when you're done."

"Really?" The eagerness seemed out of character for him, and he quickly reverted to the more casual indifference she'd picked up on earlier. "You're the first one besides me to see it this way. I figured you'd say something polite and leave it at that."

She was about to respond when a glint of something at the front of the church caught her artist's eye. Moving carefully around the holes in the floor, she walked toward a section of wall sporting a faded painting of Jesus and some of his followers on a wood panel. It was classic Americana, more cute than beautiful, but it was the raised nature of the panel that had her curiosity humming.

Scott sauntered up behind her, and she asked, "Did you notice this up here?"

"Sure," he replied with a shrug. "Why?"

"Not the painting," she clarified, nudging the frame away from the wall to reveal a shard of something that looked suspiciously like red glass. "This."

"There's no opening on the outside, so I didn't even know it was there. Hang on a sec."

He hurried over to a battered toolbox, and she couldn't help noticing that while it looked ancient, every tool was laid precisely in its place. It reminded her of her mammoth selection of paints, all arranged in order up the spectrum, and the paintbrushes of various styles she kept beside them. It seemed she and this handsome hermit both treated their tools like precious gems. Interesting.

Using a metal pry bar, he worked his way around the bottom half of the frame, then climbed on a ladder to do the top. When there were only a few points still attached, from his perch he instructed, "You hold the bottom, I'll steady it up here so we don't damage anything. Ready?"

Grasping the bottom near the corners, Jenna braced herself for the weight. "Ready."

Once they'd lowered it to the floor, she stepped back for a look at what they'd uncovered. She thought her jaw might have actually hit the floor, but she couldn't help herself.

Scott let out a low whistle. "That's incredible."

Jenna couldn't do anything more than nod. There, set into the wall of the decaying old chapel, was a stained-glass depiction of what could only be the Garden of Eden. Some of the lead dividers holding the glass shards in place were cracked or missing, leaving gaps in the colorful design that managed to shine through decades of grime. Going closer, she gently brushed away some of the dirt, admiring the depth of the greens and blues. It was humbling to consider the tremendous patience it must have taken some long-ago craftsman to fit together the tiny pieces that made up the birds and flowers.

"Who did this?" she asked in a reverent whisper.

"I dunno. Gram might, though, or know how we can find out. We should ask her."

"I can't believe it's mostly intact, after all this time." Glancing around the abandoned church, she added, "It's like getting a gift from God, isn't it?"

Scott didn't respond to that, and out of the corner of her eye she caught his grimace. Turning to face him, she asked, "Did I say something wrong?"

"I'm just thinking we should figure out how to get this thing outta here before the roof caves in on it."

"Good point." Instinct told her there was more to his reaction than he was letting on, but it wasn't her place to force him into discussing something he was clearly intent on keeping to himself. In the past year, she'd learned the Barrett men were stubborn to the core. They didn't do anything against their considerable will, and she doubted that anything she might say would change this one.

Outside, they pulled a few of the old clapboards from the structure and discovered that whoever had covered the window had nailed up a piece of wood to protect it. So with Jenna inside steadying the fragile piece, Scott used a circular saw to cut out a square slightly bigger than the glass. Then she ran out to hold the frame while he made the last cuts, and together they lowered it to the ground.

Tufts of grass stuck through the open spots, completely ruining any aesthetic effect it once had. Jenna plunked her hands on her hips in disgust. "Well, that's heartbreaking. I've never done stained glass like this, so I have no idea how to go about matching those colors."

"Whattya mean?" Scott asked, clearly confused.

"We need to restore this and hang it back where it belongs," she explained patiently.

"Why?"

"Because that's how it was meant to be." His baffled expression made it plain he still wasn't following her line of reasoning. Reaching for an explanation he might understand, she said, "It's like you making bead board for the kitchen. They have this really cool invention now, y'know. It's called Sheetrock, and it works great for building interior walls. You can paint it and everything."

"All right, you got me," he relented with a chuckle. After a moment, he sobered, and that lingering sorrow clouded his face. "I'm sure Granddad would want the chapel the way it used to be. The problem is it's gonna take most of my budget to fix the structural stuff, and I don't have a lot of cash to throw around for doodads. How much do you think it'd cost to restore this thing?"

"If you help me get it to and from my studio, I'll do it for free," she blurted impulsively. Busy as she already was, taking on another project—a free one at that—made no sense at all. But in her heart she knew it was the right thing to do. When he gave her a dubious look, she added, "For Will."

While he considered that, some of the darkness lifted from his features, and he offered his hand to seal the deal. "For Will."

They stood that way for a few seconds, hands joined as they stared at each other. She noticed a hint of warmth in the depths of his eyes, and Jenna felt herself inexplicably drawn to this broken man who was trying to rebuild his life much like the property he'd inherited. She couldn't help wondering if Will had intended just that, giving his wayward grandson another path to follow than the errant one he'd chosen.

Thinking about the generous man still made her teary, so she pulled her hand back and tried to focus her wandering mind on what needed to be done. While she was mulling, she spotted an ancient Ford delivery truck parked under a nearby tree. Decades of use had left the burgundy paint dull and faded, and she could barely read the Barrett's Sawmill logo on the door. "Don't tell me you ended up with the old mill truck."

"Yeah, it's my turn. Paul used it when he first came back, then Jason. It's not fancy, but it runs. Most of the time," he added with a wry grin.

"My van's over at the cemetery. If you can give me a lift, I'll drive it back here so we can put the window in back."

"Actually, the other day I found some old quilts in the attic of the house. We can wrap the window in those and lay it flat in the bed of the truck. It should travel well enough that way, then I'll drive you back to get your van."

His suggestion made the task easier for her but required more effort from him, she realized. She approved his gesture with a smile. "Works for me."

He retrieved the blankets, and they worked together to cushion the priceless artwork for its short trip across the valley.

Once it was secured in the back of his truck, she strolled over to eye the area beneath the hole they'd just made. "I'm guessing there are pieces of glass in the cavity between the interior and exterior walls."

Scott groaned. "Sure, tiny ones that broke when they fell outta the frame. You won't be able to repair them."

"But I can get the original colors from them," she argued, refusing to let his pessimistic assessment drown her enthusiasm for this project. "If you want this place to look the way it's supposed to, having an accurate history of the decor will be important."

"Decor. You sound like my new sisters-in-law."

Biting back a sharp comment, she deflected his criticism with her sweetest smile. "What a nice thing to say. Chelsea and Amy are two of my favorite people."

After a moment, his bravado faded a bit. "Yeah, I can see why. I didn't mean to insult your friends."

He clearly meant it as an apology, and she decided to take it that way. "They're both great people, and if you take the time to get to know them, you won't be sorry. After all, they're part of your family now."

Her gentle suggestion seemed to curdle the air between them, and the wariness he'd shown earlier returned with a cool vengeance. "Thanks for the tip," he replied in a tone edged with sarcasm.

"Oh, don't even bother with that," she scolded, glaring up at him. "Growl and sulk all you want, but I've dealt with way tougher customers than you. You don't scare me for a minute."

As he studied her intently, his expression shifted from detached to fascinated in a heartbeat. "Tougher than me? When?"

"That's absolutely none of your business," she informed him, pivoting on her heel to grab another crowbar from his immaculate toolbox. "Now, do you want to help me or am I taking this wall apart by myself?"

He didn't reply, and it took all her willpower not to look over her shoulder to gauge his reaction. Doing her best to forget he was even there, she inserted the bar into the rough-cut opening and started prying the dry, cracked boards away from the studs. Before long, Scott appeared beside her, and she braced herself for an arrogant masculine lecture on what she was doing wrong.

Instead, he silently took a position on the other side and began dismantling that section. She'd never have pegged him as the kind of guy who'd let a woman take the lead in anything, and she was more than a little impressed by his accepting attitude.

Of course, he also had a peculiar knack for aggravating her, she reminded herself immediately. Since he was a Barrett, she felt safe assuming his mulish disposition was equal parts inherited and acquired from his punishing recent history. She'd always had a weakness for bad boys, searching for the good in them and more often than not ending up disappointed when she found there wasn't enough to work with.

It was just as well, she knew. Once she finished her current backlog of projects, she'd be pulling up stakes and joining the circuit of art fairs that made their way through the region every summer. Her allotted year in Barrett's Mill was almost over, and it was time to move on. Usually, she looked forward to packing up and heading someplace else filled with new people and experiences.

Unfortunately, this time she wasn't as enthusiastic about her upcoming adventure as she'd been in the past. Sometimes being a gypsy was a lot harder than it looked.

When they pulled in at Jenna's studio, there was a familiar beat-up SUV already in the gravel parking lot.

"Were you expecting my mom this morning?" Scott asked as they got out of her van.

"No, but I'm always happy to see her," Jenna replied with a quick laugh. "When she drops by, she either has something yummy and homemade or a new customer for me."

"Now I remember where I saw your name," he said as he waited to open the car door for his mother. She was talking animatedly on her cell phone, so he went on. "Mom and Dad have a painting of yours in their living room."

"I did the original for Will last fall," Jenna explained with a melancholy smile. "His cancer got so bad, he really couldn't move around on his own anymore. He missed going for his walks, so I went out to one of his routes and took some photos, then did up a landscape of the area for him. Your parents liked it so much I painted another one for them. Your dad told me whenever he looks at it, he feels like his father's still here."

Only he wasn't, and Scott swallowed hard around the lump that suddenly clogged his throat. It frequently returned when someone mentioned Granddad, and Scott had no idea how to make it stop. Maybe it never would. Pushing aside the depressing thought, he said, "It was nice of you to do that for them. I know it's a little late, but thank you."

"For what?"

"Being so good to my family. Most people I know couldn't care less about anyone they're not related to."

That earned him a long, assessing look. "I think you've been hanging out with the wrong kind of people."

He gave a short laugh, then realized she wasn't trying to be humorous. Seeking to cover his harsh reaction, he dredged up a crooked smile. "That's pretty obvious, wouldn't you say?"

"What's obvious?" his mother asked through the window she'd lowered when he wasn't paying attention.

"That it's good to be home," he answered smoothly, opening the door for her. Since her hands were empty, he assumed that meant she was bringing Jenna more work. Which was interesting if the lady was intent on leaving soon. Maybe there was more going on than he understood. It certainly wouldn't be the first time. Kissing Mom's cheek, he asked, "What're you up to today?"

"Nothing much. Running around mostly."

Dressed in her usual jeans and a simple blouse, she didn't look like someone who ran herd over a large family and teen centers in both Barrett's Mill and nearby Cambridge. Her dark eyes snapped with intelligence and the irrepressible humor that charmed everyone she met within ten seconds. More than once, Scott had wished he had more of her in him.

Turning to Jenna, she smiled. "I actually came by to ask you a favor. Before you answer," she cautioned with a hand in the air, "take some time to think it over. It might not seem like much to you, but it could mean everything to someone else."

"Someone young and in trouble, you mean." When Mom nodded, Jenna's eyes softened with compassion. "Fill me in."

"Gretchen Lewis came to the Barrett's Mill center yesterday after school. She and her father just moved here. He works at the power plant and also in one of those quick-stop marts out on the highway, trying to keep his head above water. From what I gather, his wife cleaned out their bank account before she took off for who-knows-where."

Her tone made it plain what she thought of that, and Scott had to chuckle. "Don't sugarcoat it, Mom. Tell us how you really feel about it."

"I'm not one to judge," she said, looking from one to the other with a determined expression. "But I was raised to believe that when things get tough, family pulls together, not away. That's never more important than when you have children to consider."

Glancing over at Jenna, Scott noticed her frown seemed deeper than it should have been for a teenage girl she'd never even met. His suspicion was confirmed when she quietly asked, "How old is Gretchen?"

"Sixteen," Mom replied in the sympathetic tone that had guided Scott and his brothers through so many of their own problems. "She's adorable and whip smart, but also timid as a mouse. She mostly keeps to herself, but I noticed her drawing and went over to see what she was working on."

Reaching into her oversize canvas bag, she pulled out a piece of paper folded in half and handed it to Jenna. When the artist opened it, Scott worried that her eyes might pop right out of her head.

"Wow."

Holding it at arm's length, she stared at it for several seconds and then passed it to him. He didn't have much of an eye for art, but he instantly recognized the Crossroads Church, complete with its modest bell tower and open entry doors. She'd drawn it looking through town toward the old chapel, and he easily recognized the trees and charming old homes that stood on either side of Main Street.

The Whistlestop Diner appeared open for business, and further up was his sister-in-law Amy's dance studio, Arabesque, complete with the unfinished section Jason was adding to the old building's living quarters. There was the Donaldson house, the Morgan place and the town square with its old-fashioned gazebo. The detail was stunning, to say the least.

"If she can do this with a pencil and paper,

imagine what she could manage with some real supplies," he commented.

"My thought exactly," his mother confirmed, giving Jenna a hopeful look. "I know you're planning to leave soon, but I was hoping you might come into the center and give her some encouragement. When I complimented her, she brushed it off like she didn't believe me. If that praise came from someone who makes her living as an artist, she might take it more seriously."

Jenna hesitated, but something told him it wasn't because she was reluctant to help. She'd put a lot of time and effort into Granddad's painting, and that combined with her volunteering to plant flowers at the cemetery told Scott she had a generous nature. So what was holding her back now? It must have been something important—and very personal. Which meant it was none of his business, but he couldn't help wondering about it all the same.

Mom didn't say anything more, and he

recognized the patient look on her face from the many times he'd been on the receiving end. While she waited, Scott realized she was treating Jenna with the same respect she had her own kids. Even when they'd messed up, the Barrett boys could always count on her to hear them out before bringing down the hammer. Because of that, she was the only person he could comfortably look in the eye these days.

And Jenna, he realized with a jolt. Why, he had no clue, but he couldn't deny it was true.

When she glanced at the drawing again, Jenna finally nodded. "Okay, I'll talk to her. When would you like me to come in?"

"Thursday," Mom answered in her usual brisk way. "She said she was coming back after school that day, and I'd love for her to meet you."

"Then I'll be there."

"That's what I like most about you, honey," Mom approved, giving her a quick hug.

"You don't stand around hemming and hawing like so many folks. When there's something that needs doing, you step in to take the reins and make things happen. Gretchen should be in around four. See you then!"

With a brisk wave, she was gone.

Chapter Three

"We can lay the window down over here," Jenna said, sweeping a pile of crumpled sketches from a nearby workbench.

In one of its previous lives, her studio had been a garage with a lofted workshop space and small bathroom above. Cramped but functional, that was where she crashed at night. The place wasn't large, but the yoga teacher who'd rented it before her had retrofitted the wide-open room with sky-lights and a bank of windows that let in a ton of natural light.

Unfortunately, they also revealed the general state of disarray she preferred to work in. Two landscapes in progress were propped on easels, with completed pieces protected in Bubble Wrap and stacked in one corner. In another, her pottery wheel held something that was beginning to resemble the terra-cotta planter a customer had requested for her front porch.

A fine coating of stone dust covered everything. After he set down the window, Scott drifted toward the garden sculpture she was working on. Tilting his head one way and then another, he finally admitted, "I give up. What's it supposed to be?"

She heard that all the time from people who didn't understand the artistic process, and she swallowed an exasperated sigh. "It's for Lila Davidson's rose garden. When it's finished, it'll be a girl gnome to match the boy one I made for her last year."

"Yeah, she always did love her gardens. She reminds me of Gram that way."

It was the first time he'd mentioned being fond of anyone outside his family, and she seized on the opportunity to encourage him to open up a little. "From what I hear, they've been friends a long time."

"Lila's husband, Hank, was Granddad's foreman at the sawmill when I was growing up," he replied as he carefully unwrapped the fragile chapel window. "The four of them were pretty close back in the day. Stood up at each other's weddings, stuff like that. I'd imagine that hasn't changed any."

"It's nice having lifelong friends like that." When he shrugged, she sensed he wasn't pleased about the direction the conversation was heading. *Prickly* didn't begin to describe this man, she groused as she picked up two corners of one of the quilts while he did the same. Walking toward him, she tried again. "So, you must be glad to be back home with your old crowd."

"I haven't seen any of 'em." Apparently, her shock was obvious, because he met her stare with a hard one of his own. "I'm not in the mood to see anyone from high school.

Me being here is awkward enough for my own family, so it'd only be worse with anyone else."

"You're not giving them much credit. I mean, I know all about what happened, and that hasn't stopped us from getting to know each other. If you gave them a chance, some of them just might surprise you."

He didn't respond to that, but his expression clearly said he doubted it. This guy would try anyone's patience, and even a natural-born optimist like Jenna had her limits. "Well, it's up to you. I appreciate you helping me get this window here. If you'll just drive me back to the cemetery, I'll be out of your hair and you can get on with your day."

Once they were finished folding, he stacked the blankets on the floor and glanced around. Shoving his hands in the back pockets of his jeans, he slanted her a hesitant look. "I'm not really in a hurry or anything. I wouldn't mind seeing what kind of stuff you make here."

So, she thought with a little grin, the hunky hermit wasn't as averse to company as he claimed to be. Maybe he'd gotten so accustomed to keeping his guard up in prison he was having a tough time adjusting to his calmer, less dangerous surroundings. If that was the case, she was more than happy to help him make the leap.

"Since I'm a freelancer, I do a little of everything. Garden gnomes," she added, pointing to the one he'd made fun of earlier. "Portraits, landscapes, pottery, whatever people want. This one—" she crossed to one of the easels "—is going to a client in Roanoke. Their golden retriever is getting on in years, and they wanted a painting of her with their grandkids to remember her by after she's gone."

Strolling over, Scott tapped the photo she'd clipped to the top corner of the easel. "They've probably got a hundred pictures of her just like this one. Why spend money on a painting?"

"You can't get the same effect out of a camera," Jenna explained patiently. "An artist can capture a lot more with different brush techniques and subtle blends of color. Photographs only show what something *looks* like, not how it feels to experience it."

He took a few seconds to digest that, and a measure of respect crept into his eyes. "Y'know, I'm not the creative type, but I totally get what you're saying. Where'd you learn that kind of thing?"

His question took her back to one of the happiest times of her life, and even though it hadn't worked out the way she'd hoped, she smiled. "I went to art school for a year after high school. One of my professors was this tiny woman who was so old she'd actually met some of the artists we studied. Anyway, she taught me that true art is more than something to be displayed on a stand or hung on a wall. It should come alive and make you feel something. Exceptional pieces inspire you to see the world in a different way than you did before."

"Interesting." Looking around the room, his keen eyes landed on a smaller canvas hung for display instead of wrapped up for a customer. It was a watercolor of a yellow Cape Cod house with a white-railed porch running the width of the front. Accented by hanging flowers and others lining a walkway made of large stones, it had a cozy, welcoming look to it. "This is really nice."

"Thanks. I painted that ages ago, when Mom and I were moving around a lot. It's my dream house."

Studying it for a few moments, he announced, "Hang a swing on the porch, it'd be just about perfect."

"That's a great idea!" She approved heartily. "I'll add that in sometime along with one for that big tree to the left. I love swings."

As he continued strolling along the outer wall of her workspace, he commented, "Most of these things are done or pretty

near it. Where are you headed when you're
done here?"

His interest in her plans amazed her, since
most of the guys she'd known were too con-
sumed with their own lives to be curious
about hers. "Usually I follow the art-show
circuit because that's where the business is.
People are out traveling, hunting for unique
souvenirs to take home with them."

A slow grin edged across his face, and he
cocked his head in a challenging pose. "You
didn't answer my question. Does that mean
you're thinking about staying in Barrett's
Mill awhile longer?"

"No," she answered reflexively. When
he lifted an eyebrow, she had to admit he'd
nailed her on this one. She'd been in this
particular town longer than any of the others she'd visited, and her mind recognized it
was time to move on. The trouble was, the
people in Barrett's Mill had embraced her,
making her feel welcome even though they
obviously thought she was a nutty artist.

"Okay, maybe I am, but only to finish the window for the chapel. It belongs there, and I'll make sure it's sound before I give it back to you."

"And then?"

"I'm not sure," she confided with a shrug. "I've got space reserved in a few art fairs, but none of that's set in stone. I usually just start driving and pick a place that looks good."

"Must be nice. I'm stuck here till my parole officer says it's okay for me to leave."

His envious tone told her the years he'd spent away from his Blue Ridge hometown were no accident. "Do you have somewhere else you want to be?"

"Anywhere but here. Ironic, huh?" he added with more than a touch of bitterness. "You want to stay, but you're leaving. I'd like nothing more than to leave, but I'm staying."

The upshot was they were both staying, at least for the near future. Of course, her ultimate decision had nothing whatsoever to do with Scott being here. The fact that they seemed to be developing some kind of friendship would only make it easier for her to work with him to finish her last job before leaving town.

So, in her usual upbeat way, she did her best to lift his spirits. "Life's funny that way, I guess."

"Yeah," he muttered in disgust. "Tell me about it."

"So tell me something," Jenna began in the curious tone he'd quickly learned to be wary of. "Does anyone ever say no to your mother?"

He made a show of thinking that over, squinting up at the beams in the ceiling. Focusing back on her, he grinned and shook his head. "Nope."

"I wonder what her secret is."

Stepping closer, he leaned in and murmured, "We're all afraid of her."

Jenna laughed at that, and it struck him that she was one of the most cheerful people he'd ever met. With a ready smile and a dry sense of humor that mirrored his own, she was sweet and fun, with a heart open enough to care about a sad teenage girl and an ex-con who'd given up on having the kind of life he wanted more than anything.

Something deep inside him that had been dead a long time began rustling, as if it was waking from a long sleep to discover the sun was shining. Much to his dismay, a single morning with Jenna Reed had him rethinking his vow to be content with his own company.

Knowing how dangerous such sentimental thoughts could be, he firmly pushed them back down where they belonged. She was leaving town in a few weeks, and after that, chances were he'd never see her again.

Considering his disastrous track record with women, knowing they'd remain friends should have eased his worries. Instead, it made him wish things could be different.

"Ready to go?" Hoping to conceal his conflicting emotions from her, he leaned down to pick up the quilts.

"In a sec." Leaving him by the door, she scampered up the open-backed steps that led up to the loft and came down with a glass dish. "Olivia sent some leftovers back with me after one of your family's Sunday dinners a couple weeks ago. Her house is on the way out to the cemetery. Would you mind stopping there real quick so I can return this?"

Scott recognized a setup when he heard one, and he gave her a long, hard stare. Most people backed up a step or two when he did that, but this woman didn't even flinch. She took it in stride, patiently waiting for him to answer her. He'd already told her more than he should have about himself, but he couldn't seem to help going a step further. "It's not that I don't want to see her."

"This isn't about you seeing her," Jenna informed him as if she had no clue what he was referring to. "It's about me returning a dish. You don't even have to get out of the truck if you don't want to."

"That'd look stupid, and you know it."

"Contrary to what you seem to believe, folks have plenty going on in their own lives without worrying about what you're up to," she retorted primly. "If you'd rather she doesn't know you're there, I won't mention it. Go inside or don't. Totally up to you."

With that, she sailed past him and out the door to his truck.

"Do you always leave your door open like this?" he shouted.

"Just pull it shut. It'll lock behind you."

Outmaneuvered for now, he followed along and joined her in the cab of the ancient pickup. Mentally crossing his fingers, he turned the key and was relieved when the engine turned over with only a mild protest.

As it settled into a throaty rumble, he pulled out onto the highway and headed for town.

Heading up Main Street, he was treated to the full-color version of Gretchen's sketch and couldn't help smiling. He hadn't experienced spring in the Blue Ridge Mountains in a long time, and he had to admit it was even prettier than he remembered. A warm breeze wafted through the open windows, scented with a combination of various flowers and the barbecue cookers out back of The Whistlestop.

Originally built from an old trolley and section of track, the town's landmark diner now boasted a modest-size dining room that served up some of the best food anywhere. He'd visited lots of places and eaten in dozens of restaurants, but for him Molly and Bruce Harkness's down-home cooking still ranked at the top.

"I love that restaurant," Jenna said, taking a long sniff of the air. "Not only can those two cook up a storm, they were my first customers when I came into town. Beyond that, Molly's the best PR I've ever had."

"Yeah, she knows everyone hereabouts," Scott agreed, recalling his grandmother's old friend with a grin. "If she likes you, you're golden."

"And if she doesn't?"

He gave a mock shudder. "I don't even wanna think about it."

On the other side of the tiny business district, he took a right into his grandparents' driveway. Well, Gram's driveway now, he amended soberly. Granddad's beloved blue sedan sat in its usual spot, its cover of dust showing it hadn't been moved recently. Parking beside it, Scott said, "Someone should take that old clunker out and make sure it'll run if she needs to use it."

"Good idea," Jenna agreed lightly as she reached for the handle. "I won't be long."

"Don't be a goose. I'm going with you." When he climbed out and walked around to open the passenger door for her, he found her smiling at him. "What?"

"You're going to make her day, you know."

"Or ruin it," he parried, suddenly uncertain about his decision to tag along. Glancing at the old farmhouse, he still could remember racing around the yard with his cousins and climbing the tall oaks that shaded the front porch. With a collection of white wicker furniture and hanging pots of bright flowers, it invited you to come up and sit for a while.

Welcoming, he thought with a frown The trouble was, he'd been gone so long he wasn't sure he belonged here anymore. While he debated with himself, the front screen door creaked open, and his grandmother stepped onto the porch. She gave him a long look, and he fought the urge to squirm the way he had when he'd been a little boy caught doing something he wasn't supposed to.

"I've got fresh snickerdoodles and lemonade," she said finally. "If you want some."

His favorite childhood snack. He couldn't imagine how she'd known to make it. Then it hit him, and he turned to Jenna. "You called her?"

"When you were hunting for those quilts," she confirmed with a poorly concealed grin.

So, the sunny artist had a devious side, he mused as he opened Jenna's door and walked up the front steps with her. Who knew? When he reached the porch, he saw tears welling in Gram's eyes and stopped dead. "What's wrong?"

"I'm just so happy to see you. It's been such a long time."

She opened her arms wide, and the last bit of his misgivings evaporated as he went into that warm embrace. He'd dreamed of it so many times, he'd begun to believe the recurring image was simply the result of being homesick. But now, standing there with her, knowing she forgave him for the mistakes he'd made, he actually could believe that somehow, someday everything would be all right.

Chapter Four

Inside the Barrett house, things were right and wrong at the same time.

Jenna hadn't been here since Will's funeral, and it still struck her as odd that the dining room had gone back to its normal configuration. During the final months of his illness, Will's hospital bed had dominated a corner of the large room, leaving space for the visitors Olivia coerced into dropping by so she and her husband wouldn't feel so isolated. Its absence only reinforced the fact that Jenna never again would see the kind old man who'd found so much joy in a simple landscape she'd painted for him.

"So nice to have company during the week," Olivia said, motioning for them to sit at the kitchen table. Donning a set of oven mitts shaped like sunflowers, she pulled a scrumptious tray of cookies from the oven in a cloud of cinnamon-sugary aroma. "Ever since Jenna called, I've been racking my brain trying to figure out how you two could possibly have met. It must be an interesting story."

After pouring three glasses of lemonade, she set the plate of cookies down and joined them with an expectant look. Jenna waited for Scott to answer her, but he was too busy shoving cookies into his mouth. Deciding it was up to her, she said, "I went out to the cemetery to plant flowers for Will, and Scott was there. So I drafted him to help me out. It turns out he's pretty good with a shovel."

"And she's pretty good at giving orders," he piped up with a chuckle. "Worked out fine."

Olivia turned an adoring look on him and patted his hand. "It can't have been easy for you, but I know your grandfather was pleased to see you. Thank you for taking the time to go out there and be with him awhile."

Misery swept across Scott's face, and he fixed her with a pleading look. "I wanted to visit sooner, Gram. I just couldn't."

"Have you been avoiding the cemetery," she asked gently, "or me?"

That tortured expression was back, only much worse than she'd seen on his face earlier. Jenna felt awkward being included in such a private moment, but she feared moving would distract him from forcing the guilt he felt out into the open. That was the first step in overcoming it, she knew, and instinct told her his compassionate but very pragmatic grandmother was the one to nudge him in the right direction.

"Both," he confided in a hoarse whisper. After swallowing some lemonade, he rested his hand over hers. "I'll always be sorry for that."

"Oh, I hope not," she told him briskly. "Such a waste of time, reliving the past over and over." Dark eyes twinkling with her characteristic optimism, she punctuated her little lesson with a fond smile. "Those times are done and gone, and now that you're home, there are plenty more good ones to come. You'll see."

"I'll take your word for it."

It took him a few seconds, but he returned the smile, and Jenna got a glimpse of what this cool, distant man must have looked like years ago, before the consequences of his bad choices had all but shut him down. She sensed there was more to it than mere happiness, and she mulled that over while the three of them chatted about the latest goings-on around town. When she finally identified what had changed Scott's mood, she couldn't help smiling.

It was trust. So he was capable of it, after all, she mused with genuine interest. Prison hadn't destroyed it, just sent it into hiding. Which, considering what he must have been through, was totally understandable. Knowing he still had the ability to believe in someone made Jenna want to find a way to make him trust her, too. She wasn't sure why his opinion of her mattered so much, but in situations like this she always listened to her intuition. Even if what it was telling her didn't make sense at the time, in the long run it was usually right.

"Here we are, rattling along, when we've got a guest at the table," Olivia said, bringing Jenna back into the conversation. "How are things at your studio?"

No one wanted to hear her life was chaotic and she was way behind on her deadlines, so she smiled and gave her usual chipper response. "Just fine. Diane stopped in this morning and asked me to drop by the teen center later this week to talk to one of the new girls about art."

"Gretchen," Olivia commented with a nod. "Such a heartbreaking story with her and her father struggling the way they are. You're just the kind of role model she needs."

"I don't think I'd be anyone's choice as a mentor," Jenna protested with a laugh. "I'm pretty sure Diane just wants me to tell Gretchen how talented she is, encourage her to keep practicing, that kind of thing."

"Like that munchkin art professor did for you," Scott suggested.

"In slightly less colorful language," she clarified with a nostalgic smile. "Miss Fontaine was—what's the word?"

"Nutty?" he asked in a helpful tone.

"Eccentric. Most creative people are."

"Oh, that's true," Olivia confirmed with a nod. "My old friend Annabelle, God rest her, sang like an angel and could play a dozen different instruments. She also talked to the coatrack in her foyer like it was a real person and couldn't remember what she was doing from one minute to the next. She was a gifted musician but madder than a hatter."

They all laughed at that, and Scott polished off the rest of his drink before standing. "I hate to leave, Gram, but I have to drop Jenna off at the cemetery so she can pick up her van. After that, I really should get back to the house. If I don't finish covering the holes in the chapel roof, that storm they're talking about is gonna wreck all the new wood I put up inside."

"Don't you dare apologize to me for being busy. I've got things to do, too," she assured him as she stood and went up on tiptoe to kiss his cheek. All her grandsons towered over her, but Jenna thought it was adorable the way Olivia still gave them a quick peck whenever they were headed out. "If you're interested, I'm making pot roast Friday night."

Grinning, he cocked his head like a half-starved hound who'd just gotten wind of a free meal. "For me?"

"Well, it's not for me," she teased, then turned to Jenna with a critical look. "I noticed you've been losing weight again, dear. I think you'd better come, too, and have something that didn't come out of a microwave. There will be plenty of food, so you two can split the leftovers."

Scott eyed her warily. "You're not trying to set us up, are you?"

"Don't be ridiculous," she chided him. "I've invited everyone who's got the night free, so there will be lots of other folks here."

"You're having a family shindig now?" he asked. "How come?"

"Because I feel like having company, and no one ever turns down my cooking." She looked from him to Jenna. "Should I plan on seeing you two or not?"

Jenna had been planning to work late to finish up the doggy painting for her clients. But since she didn't have a domestic bone in her body, she never could resist the lure of a home-cooked meal. "Sounds good to me. Six o'clock?"

Olivia gave her grandson a questioning look, and after hesitating, he gave in with a grin. "Works for me. While I'm here, I'll tighten up that loose railing on your front steps."

She beamed at him as if he'd just offered to build her a whole new porch. "That would be wonderful, honey. Thank you."

"I'd imagine there's a lot more jobs like that around here," he commented as she walked Jenna and him to the door. "I know Paul and Jason have their hands full with the mill, so you go ahead and make a list. It might take me a while, but I'll make sure everything gets done."

"I'll do that." Pausing on the porch, she hugged him again, grasping his arms as she gazed up at him. "Welcome home, Scott."

His sheepish grin made him look about ten years old, and he stooped to kiss her cheek. "Thanks, Gram. See you Friday."

Back in the truck, Jenna couldn't help gloating a little. "So, that went well."

"As blatant manipulation goes, it was a ten." While he fiddled with the ignition, he sighed. "But I can't blame you for taking a shot. I wasn't getting anywhere on my own, but now I feel stupid for being so worried about seeing her."

"Your grandmother is a very forgiving person," Jenna reminded him gently. "Actually, your whole family's like that. It's one of the big reasons I enjoy spending time with them. They don't expect anyone to be perfect, and that makes it easier for me to be myself."

"Mostly, they don't have patience for a lot of nonsense." When the ancient truck finally let out a hacking cough and started, Scott pulled out of the driveway and headed out of town. "Mom sees right through that kinda thing, and she seems to think a lot of you. That's good enough for me."

"Good to know."

"So, what've you got planned for Gretchen?"

"No plans," she replied with a shrug. "I'll let her run the show. If she wants to confide in me, I'll listen. If not, that'll be okay, too. She's old enough to decide stuff like that for herself."

Slanting her a look, Scott opened his mouth to speak, then shut it again. His reserve came across to her as more of a habit than part of his real personality, and she seized the opportunity to take another whack at this very stubborn nut. "You wanted to ask me something?"

"None of my business."

"That never stops anyone else," she informed him with a laugh. "What did you want to know?"

Another hesitation, then very quietly he asked, "What happened with you and your mom?"

Jenna's heart thudded to a stop. Of all the things he could have questioned her about, her mother was the last one she'd anticipated. In the past year, the only person she'd confessed her sordid history to was Diane Barrett, and then only with a lot of patient— and persistent—encouragement.

Keeping secrets, that one especially, had become a bad tendency for her. Gradually, she'd come to recognize that it served no purpose other than to lead her in never-ending circles back to a time in her life she was trying desperately to leave behind her. But Scott had been forthright with her about his own past, she reminded herself. It was only fair for her to do the same.

"It's not a nice story," she cautioned him.

"I kinda figured that when I saw your reaction to what my mom said about Gretchen's mother taking off." Pulling onto the graveled shoulder of the road, he swiveled to face her squarely. "You looked upset, but you covered it up pretty fast. It's been bugging me ever since."

"Why?"

He shrugged, his baffled expression a perfect mirror for the one she must be wearing right now. "Just curious, I guess. You don't have to tell me if you don't want to."

"No, it's okay," she said, as much to convince herself as him. Figuring it was best to get this over with, she dived right in. "For as long as I can remember, it was just Mom and me. She had lots of boyfriends, but none of them stayed for long. We moved around a lot, which made it tough to get attached to people, never knowing when we'd be leaving."

"Not a very nice way to grow up," he commented in a critical tone. "Kids need a place to call home."

So do adults, Jenna added silently before going on. "Anyway, when I was sixteen, we were living in Dayton, Ohio. One day after school I went to my friend Vicky's house for a sleepover. When they dropped me off the next morning, our car was gone and the only things left in the house were mine. No note, nothing."

She heard the disgust in her voice as the resentment she'd carried with her all these years raged to the surface. Taking a deep breath, she did her best to let it go through her and out the way the school counselor had taught her. Even now it was easier said than done, but she still made the attempt because she didn't know what else to do.

Scott's eyes darkened in a threatening way that would have scared her if she hadn't understood his anger wasn't aimed at her. "What happened then?"

"Vicky's dad was a cop, so he got the police involved right away. But it didn't matter," she added bitterly. "Mom was long gone, and they never found a trace of her. You'd think it wouldn't be too hard to track down someone named Anastasia Reed, but I guess she went off the grid or something. Fortunately, Vicky's parents stepped up and became my foster family so I could finish high school there. I was a pretty good student, and I got a scholarship to a local university. Except for my art class, college wasn't my thing, so after a year I quit that and went out on my own."

The story of her life spilled out with a swiftness that astonished her. In a way, that was good because it was over quickly. It was also bad, because at her age it should take her longer to recount her personal history. Why didn't it? she wondered, then shoved the unanswerable question aside for another time. For now, she focused on the shifting expressions moving across Scott's face. Some, such as sympathy, she understood. Others, not so much. Those were the ones that intrigued her the most, even though she had a feeling they weren't exactly uplifting.

Just when she thought he might not say

anything at all, he surprised her with a warm smile. "You know helping Gretchen will bring out all those bad memories for you, but you're willing to do it anyway. Except for my family, I didn't think people like you still existed."

"We're around," she assured him, relieved that he seemed to accept her, ragged past and all. "You just have to keep your mind open enough to recognize us when we pop up in front of you."

"I have to say," he began as he pulled back onto the road. "You're one of the most optimistic folks I've ever met. With what happened to you when you were young, how do you manage that?"

Picking up on the opportunity to offer this drowning man a lifeline, Jenna smiled. "Faith."

His eyes flicked to her before returning to the road. "In people or God?"

"Both."

"Don't tell me," he grumbled. "You're one

of those folks who thinks there's something good in everyone."

"Yup. It can be buried pretty far down sometimes, but if you keep digging you'll find it."

The corners of his mouth dipped into a frown. "What about your mom?"

That one was tougher, but with a lot of prayer, Jenna had slowly but surely come to an uneasy sort of understanding about her absent mother. "She was a fabulous artist. Giving life to her ideas was what mattered most to her."

More than once over the years, Jenna had wondered if Anastasia Reed had regretted being saddled with the daughter she'd brought into the world. Another question with no answer. Unfortunately, where her mother was concerned, Jenna had enough of them to drive anyone bonkers.

"Do you think you were better off with your foster family than with your mother?" Scott asked as he drove around the curve that ended at a small parking lot outside the cemetery.

No one had ever thought to ask her that, and she considered his question carefully before responding, "In some ways I was. I got to stay in one place for two whole years, went to my prom and graduated with honors. They were a nice, normal family, and they gave me the kind of stability Mom couldn't seem to manage. I think I made out pretty well."

They'd reached the tall iron gates that bracketed the lane leading into the cemetery, and Scott parked next to her van. Climbing out of the truck, he came around to open her door for her. She'd have to check her map for other sleepy towns to visit below the Mason-Dixon line, she thought with a grin. These Southern-gentleman manners had really grown on her.

Giving her a long, thoughtful look, he said, "I know we just met this morning, but something tells me you'd make out well no matter what life threw at you."

"You can do anything," she replied, paraphrasing one of her favorite Bible verses. "You just need a little faith."

"Is that your personal philosophy, or are you trying to convince me it'll work for me, too?"

"Yes."

He barked out a derisive laugh, but she resolutely held her ground and returned that skeptical stare with a determined one of her own. He was a tough customer, no doubt about that, but she had yet to meet someone she couldn't connect with if she kept searching for a way in. It might take a while with Scott, but her gut was telling her he was worth the effort.

As they continued their staring contest, his eyes narrowed with something akin to respect. "You're not afraid of me, are you?"

"Not even a teeny, tiny bit. I think you growl and glare to make people stay away because you don't know how else to keep yourself safe. But you're here now," she reminded him firmly. "You don't have to stand on your own anymore."

"It's a hard habit to break," he confided in a hushed voice laced with remorse. "I'm not sure I can do it."

"You're a smart guy, Scott. You can do anything you set your mind to."

"How could you possibly think that? You hardly know me."

"I know your family," she told him with a smile. "And how much they love you, how much they missed you while you were gone. They're all ready to support you and help you make a better future for yourself."

After chewing on that for a minute, he said, "I'm not sure I deserve their help."

"Everyone deserves a second chance. This town is full of good people who believe that and would be willing to give you a fresh start." Resting a hand on his arm, she added, "You just have to let them do it."

That got her a wan smile, and as he pulled away from her, she couldn't tell if she'd gotten through to him or not. At least he'd listened to her little sermon, she thought as she said goodbye and headed for her van.

It might not seem like much right now, but it was a start.

When he got back to the chapel, Scott stood in the middle of the floor trying to figure out what was bugging him. Except for the hole he'd hacked in the wall to rescue the window, nothing had changed as far as he could see. Then he realized the difference wasn't visual.

It was quiet.

So quiet, he could hear birds chirping in the trees outside and the distant rumble of thunder heading in from the west. Jenna had been here less than an hour, but during her short stay, he'd gotten accustomed to hearing the sound of a human voice. And liked it, he admitted grudgingly. Apparently, a week of having only himself for company was wearing thin.

After hammering a temporary filler into the wall where the stained-glass window had been, he climbed onto the roof and covered the worrisome holes to keep out the rain. Old country music on the radio didn't do much to fill the echoing space, and he decided to take a stroll before the rain started. He left the chapel and went into the house to get a few pieces of old bead board from the pile in what used to be the parlor. There was so much to do around the old place, he figured it wouldn't matter much if he took some time out for an errand.

Now that he could do pretty much whatever he wanted, he took full advantage of the freedom to splash across Sterling Creek and head for the sawmill a long-ago Barrett had founded to help rebuild the town after the Civil War. Following the creek while it bubbled along, he let himself relax enough to appreciate his peaceful surroundings.

Centuries-old trees flanked him on both sides, their leafy canopies throwing dapples of sunlight onto the stream and the path his brother's bloodhound had worn beside it. Scott paused to allow a mama beaver and her brood of four skitter down the bank in front of him and disappear under their dam. That was the kind of thing he recalled from his childhood, when Granddad would take them all for a nature walk and a lesson on how precious the land and creatures surrounding them were.

Someday, Scott hoped he'd be able to think of his grandfather and smile instead of frown. For now, he let the sadness wash over him, mimicking the current running alongside the path. The brook had been following this exact same route for generations before Scott, and would still be around long after he was gone. Winding its way through the forest, bringing water to the trees and animals before continuing on its way to do more of the same downstream.

The steadiness of that was comforting to him, and he felt some of the sorrow he'd been dragging around with him lift away. It was a relief to let it go, and his steps felt lighter as he picked up the sound of the mill's running waterwheel on the breeze.

As he rounded the last bend in the creek, he got the attention of a keen canine nose and braced himself as his brother's insane bloodhound raced toward him at full speed. The dog barreled into Scott, then retreated almost immediately, running in circles while he flung his head back and bayed at the top of his lungs.

"Hey there, Boyd. We just met the other day, so I wasn't sure you'd remember me."

He leaned down to ruffle the dog's floppy ears and heard his older brother Paul laughing. "Remember you? From the looks of it, he's been dying to see you again."

"It's nice to be missed, I guess."

Scott cringed at the hesitance he noticed in his voice, but Paul ignored it and eyed the slender pieces of wood he'd carried over. "Whatcha got there?"

"Original slats from the homestead kitchen," Scott explained, holding them on the palms of his hands so Paul could get a better look. "The other night, you said you've got some scrap oak piling up over here. I'm hoping it's a decent match."

"And free," he filled in with a grin. "Right?"

"Well, no," Scott stammered, caught off guard by the unexpected response. "I can pay you for it."

"Your money's no good here," Paul corrected him, slinging an arm around his shoulders in a big-brother gesture. They began walking toward the mill house, and he added, "I'm glad you came by. I've got a job that's beyond me, and I could use your help."

Two people in one day, Scott mused, three if he counted Jenna. For someone who'd gotten used to getting by completely on his own, this helping-hand thing would take some getting used to. "With what?"

"You know Chelsea and I bought the old Garrison house on Ingram Street."

"Can't imagine why," he scoffed. "That place has been on its last legs for years."

"It's a project, that's for sure," Paul agreed with a chuckle. "The thing is, I'm good with furniture, garden benches, things like that. I'm not much for built-in stuff, and Chelsea's got her heart set on re-creating the breakfront that used to be in our dining room. She has this vision in her head of us hosting everyone there during the holidays, and she says it won't be right without that piece there the way it should be."

"What happened to the original?"

"Went to auction years ago to help pay off Mr. Garrison's medical bills. It's probably in some rich guy's mansion in Roanoke now."

That struck Scott the wrong way, and when they stopped near the front steps leading up into the mill office, he scowled. "I get tired of people tearing things apart and only taking what they want. Fix it or leave it alone. Don't take only the parts you want and leave the rest behind to rot."

As soon as the words left his mouth, he realized they could be misconstrued by anyone with half a brain. He hadn't meant to spin a metaphor about himself, but somehow he'd managed it anyway.

"That's how we feel about it, too," Paul told him, his dark eyes glittering with the same appreciation for the home's past. "So, whattya think?"

"I'd rather take a look at it before I start making promises," Scot hedged. "I don't suppose you've got any pictures?"

"No, but the rest of the woodwork in the house looks original," a female voice suggested from the porch. Scott looked up to find Paul's wife, Chelsea, in the doorway, a sleeping orange tiger cat cradled in her arms like a child. "You might be able to get some ideas from that."

Scott was intrigued by the idea, but he'd learned the hard way that going out on a limb had the very real potential for ending in disaster. While failing on his own wasn't the worst thing in the world, he was hesitant to ruin Paul and Chelsea's dining room. He was pretty sure they didn't want that, either.

After he and Paul joined her on the porch, Scott said, "Historical restoration isn't exactly my specialty. You'd do better to find a pro."

"Pros are expensive," Chelsea reminded him in a firm but sweet tone that probably worked wonders on his stubborn older brother. "Not to mention, booked up for a year in advance. I want the buffet done in time for us to have the whole family at our place for Christmas."

Scott opened his mouth to ask her why, and then it hit him. How she was holding her cat, the way Paul was standing behind her, his arms wrapped protectively around her. "You're having a baby, aren't you?"

"Told you he was sharp," her husband said with a chuckle. "We're telling the family Friday night at Gram's. Act surprised," he added with a stern look.

"No problem." Scott leaned against one of the roof supports, gazing over at the happy couple. Crossing his arms, he tried to envision them as parents and was surprised to find it wasn't as difficult as it should have been. "I probably won't be over the shock by then, anyway. Congratulations, by the way."

Even to his own ears, the good wishes sounded like a lame afterthought, and he tried to come up with a way to smooth over his misstep. The gesture was totally out of character for him, but he forced himself to embrace them both. It felt stiff and awkward to him, but in the end he was glad he'd made the effort.

Chelsea gave him a warm smile and said, "I picked up sandwiches for the crew, and there are some left in the fridge if you want them."

"Really? That must mean Jason's not here," he joked.

"He had lunch in town with Amy today," she explained. "The newlyweds are trying to agree on paint colors for the kitchen he just finished. Are you hungry?"

"Us Barrett boys are always hungry," he informed her as he opened the door and stepped back to let them go through.

"Yeah," she replied with a raised eyebrow for Paul. "Tell me about it."

Chapter Five

Scott was totally out of nails.

He couldn't believe it, but then realized he'd used the last of them cobbling the sad excuse for a roof back together. Once he started taking inventory, he discovered he was dangerously low on a lot of other things. Including money.

The fund Granddad had set up for restoring the chapel was administered by an old lawyer friend of his who was currently out of town visiting his daughter and her family. While he'd told Scott to call him anytime, Scott didn't want to interrupt his family visit to ask him for a check to cover the supplies he needed. The same man was in charge of doling out money for his living expenses, which left Scott with the cash he had in his wallet until he could get more.

If he didn't have something to do, he feared he'd lose his mind out here in the woods all alone. Inspiration struck, and he thumbed to the sawmill's number on his phone. "Hi, Chelsea. Is Paul around?"

Apparently he was in the office because he came on the line within a couple of seconds. "What's up, woodchuck?"

"Y'know, I hated that when we were kids," he growled back.

Totally unfazed, his irritating big brother chuckled. "Yeah, I seem to recall that."

Being mad about it was getting him absolutely nowhere, so he decided to chill out and get to the point. "I need some stuff here at the homestead, and I'm out of cash till Granddad's lawyer comes back next week.

I was hoping I could use the mill account at Stegall's Hardware and then pay you back."

"Sure, but you don't have to reimburse me. It's your money, too."

"Are you sure? It's not like I work at the mill," Scott pointed out.

"You will if I need you," Paul promised with another chuckle. "When the holidays roll around we get swamped with orders, and it's all hands on deck."

While it was masked with humor, Scott recognized what his brother was doing and couldn't hold back a rare surge of hope. Swallowing to keep his voice steady, he asked, "Are you offering me a job?"

"If you want it. There's always a spot for a good carpenter around here."

Paul hadn't phrased it like someone trying to bail out a family member who was down on his luck, Scott noted with gratitude. He'd spoken like a prospective employer who was always on the lookout for good people. If one of them happened to be named Barrett, that was fine. "Thanks for the offer. I'll keep it in mind."

"Good. Don't let that roof cave in while you're up there, okay?"

"Gotcha," he replied with a laugh. "Later."

After making a quick list, Scott got the ancient truck running on the fourth try and headed into town. At one end of the modest business district, he parked out front of Stegall's Hardware and glanced around to see who else was out this morning. Fred Morgan drove past in his tow truck, raising a hand to Scott in greeting. People on the sidewalk outside the post office had varying reactions, though.

One couple smiled and returned his "good morning," while their companions stared straight through him as if he wasn't even there. They all knew his parents, and he'd gone to school with their kids right here in Barrett's Mill. It was to be expected, he supposed, but the rejection still stung. Hoping for a better result, he pushed open the glass front door of the shop and went inside.

The store itself hadn't changed much since his childhood. He used to come here with Dad and Granddad, admiring the saws and lathes, listening while they talked wood-working and construction with his grand-father's old friend Joe Stegall. Today, a younger man stood beside the counter, an electronic gadget dangling from his belt and a polite smile frozen on his face. "Good morning. Can I help you?"

"I hope so." He extended his hand. "Scott Barrett."

From the hesitant way the guy accepted his gesture, he knew perfectly well who Scott was. Nervously licking his lips, he said, "Alan Pullman. Nice to meet you."

Clearly a lie, but there was nothing Scott could do about it, so he pulled out his list and did his best to sound friendly. "I'm working on the old house and chapel out on Mill Road. I'm hoping you've got all this stuff in stock."

Alan scanned the list and nodded. "We should be able to fill this without a problem. Did you want everything delivered?"

"No, I'll take it with me. I've got plenty of room in the truck."

Again, the man hesitated, and Scott folded his hands in front of him, hoping to appear as nonthreatening as possible. Then it hit him what the problem was: Alan was working alone. If he went out back to fill the order that would leave Scott unsupervised with all those expensive tools.

It really wasn't his fault, Scott had to admit. If their roles had been reversed, he wouldn't trust an ex-con in his store, either. So he did something he seldom did with anyone. He tried to compromise. "Tell you what? Why don't you bring it out, after all? I'll be around all day."

"That'll work," Alan agreed quickly. Stepping behind the counter, he began punching stock numbers into the computer. When he had a total, he asked, "How did you want to pay?"

"Paul said it was okay for me to use the mill account."

Wrong answer. Alan's helpful attitude imploded, and he eyed Scott suspiciously. "Really? He's never done that for anyone before."

"This is different. I'm his brother."

"That doesn't matter."

"You really think I'd try to rip off my family's business?"

"I don't know what you'd try," Alan retorted. "But I do know you're not on the approved list for charging to the account we have for Barrett's Sawmill."

Scott had taken more than enough of this pencil neck's condescending attitude. It was a good thing there was a wide counter between them, or things might have gotten ugly. Still, he pulled himself up to his full height and leaned his hands on the glass case filled with knives of various sizes. It put them almost nose to nose, and he was just mean enough to be pleased when the other man shrank back in fear.

"There you are!" a familiar voice called out from the front door. "I've been looking all over for you. Did you forget you're taking me to lunch?"

The woman had incredible timing, Scott thought as Jenna hustled over to join them. She'd broken through his furious haze, and out of respect for her, he wrestled his temper back under control and stood down. No doubt, he now owed her lunch, but considering she'd just saved him from making a complete fool of himself, he figured he was getting off cheap.

"Sorry about that. We're almost finished here, I think," he added, willing the clerk to agree with him. Fortunately, he did, but his wide-eyed nod clearly said Scott had made his point.

"Good morning, Alan," she chirped like a bluebird without a care in the world. "How's Valerie doing these days?"

"Fine, thanks. What can I get you?"

Giving him a playful wink, she pointed at Scott's list. "That'll be enough for now. I forgot to eat breakfast, so I'm famished."

"Those supplies are for you?"

"Well, not directly, but Scott and I are working on the chapel project together. Didn't he mention that?" she asked in a tone sweet enough to keep a dentist in business for months.

"No, he didn't. But he wanted to charge these materials to the mill account."

She blinked in apparent confusion. Man, she was good.

"Is that a problem?" she asked innocently. "I mean, he's a Barrett, isn't he?"

"Well, yeah. But he's not on the list."

"Of course not," Scott growled. "I just got back into town."

"I'm sure you can straighten this out, Alan," Jenna said, soothing Scott's temper with a hand on his arm. "Why don't you go call Paul from the office and get his authorization for this stuff? We'll wait here."

Alan's eyes flicked apprehensively to Scott, who kept his voice low to avoid yelling in frustration. "I promise to keep my hands off the register."

"I'm sorry," the guy stammered. "It's just—"

"Go make your call," Jenna nudged, adding a smile for good measure. "He understands."

When Alan had scampered away, Scott glowered at his defender. "For the record, I do *not* understand."

Waving off his anger with a graceful sweep of her hand, she fixed him with a warning look. "You have to stop snarling

at people. It just makes things tougher on
you."

"He's a narrow-minded, intolerant, sanc-
timonious—"

"Ooh, good word. Let me write that one
down."

She started digging through her beat-up
leather messenger bag and then angled an
aggravating smirk up at him. This smart-
aleck artist was getting on his last nerve,
but she was going to an awful lot of trouble
to lighten him up. He appreciated the effort
she was making on his behalf, even though
she probably was wasting her time. So he
flipped over his list and gave her the pen
from his pocket.

"Thanks. Now, how do you spell that?"
While he rattled off the letters, she made
quite a show of following along. When he
finished, she held the paper out and stared
at it with a quizzical look. "How 'bout that?
It's spelled just like it sounds."

Scott burst into laughter. He couldn't help

it, especially when she gave him what he could only describe as a Cleopatra smile. Coy with more than a hint of mystery, it made him want to learn more about what made this enchanting woman tick.

A lot more.

Fortunately, Alan returned in time to derail that very dangerous train of thought.

"I honestly apologize for hassling you, Scott. Paul cleared everything up."

Judging by the man's pale complexion, Paul had done a good deal more than that, and Scott made a mental note to thank his big brother for having his back. There were advantages to being home, after all. Figuring the poor guy had taken enough of a beating, he opted to take the high road. Offering his hand again, he was relieved when Alan took it without pause. "No hard feelings."

"It won't happen again, I promise."

"I'm sure it won't."

Alan's previous condescension had given

way to customer-service mode, and he asked, "When would you like these things delivered?"

"Actually, I think I'm gonna take the rest of today off, so tomorrow's fine."

What? Scott almost turned around to see who'd said those words, then realized he had. He didn't want to come across as some kind of lunatic, so he ignored Jenna's shocked look and let the clerk finish his tallying in silence.

When they were outside the store, Jenna turned to him with a bewildered expression. "You're taking today off? Seriously?"

"Something smells good at The Whistlestop," he replied, avoiding the painfully obvious answer to her question. "That work for you?"

Looking across the street, Jenna skimmed the busy dining room at the landmark diner and came back to him with a dubious look.

"You really think it's a good idea for you to be going in there when it's so crowded?"

"Gonna have to do it sooner or later," he reasoned, ushering her across the street with a hand resting lightly on her back. "If you're sitting with me, it might be almost tolerable."

So, that was it, she thought sadly. He wanted her to accompany him as a shield, so folks wouldn't be as hard on him as Alan Pullman had been. While she understood people's reticence to welcome Scott back with open arms, part of her couldn't help wondering if he'd ever be able to overcome his past and rebuild his life in this tiny, close-knit community. Maybe he had the right idea about starting fresh somewhere else. She'd certainly done it often enough.

When they reached the front door, he opened it and stood aside for her to go through. Just one more thing to miss when she left for the fair circuit, she thought wistfully. Unlike so many other places she'd been, around here people still took the time to be courteous to each other. Not that she wasn't perfectly capable of opening her own doors, of course. It was just nice to be treated like a lady, even when she was dressed in threadbare denim and splotches of drying clay.

Dozens of eyes swung to them and Scott muttered, "Wonderful."

"Now, don't be that way. Folks always look up like that when someone comes inside. They're curious about who's here for lunch."

"You mean nosy," he corrected her darkly. "Probably trying to figure out what you're doing hanging out with me."

Chances were he was right, but she wasn't about to let his pessimism ruin such a nice day. "I make it a rule not to eat with nasty people. It's bad for my digestion. If you're gonna stick with the doom-and-gloom routine, you can go sit over there."

Pointing at a tiny one-person booth in the corner usually reserved for staff meal breaks, she was rewarded with a low chuckle. Not exactly laughter, but it was a vast improvement over grumbling. "Okay, I'll behave."

"Good boy."

"Well, now, look who finally decided to come by and see me!" Molly Harkness shouted a greeting from the end of the lunch counter. Hurrying over, she hugged Jenna quickly, saving a much longer one for Scott. Molly looked tiny standing next to him, but he accepted her attention with a grateful smile. Pulling away, she grasped his arms and beamed up at him. "I'm so glad you dropped in. I was starting to think you'd learned how to cook or some such thing."

"Not a bit. What smells so good in here?"

"Everything," she replied with a bright laugh. "A table for two just freed up by the front window. I'll have Rachel pick up some silverware and menus and meet you there."

When they were sitting down, Jenna leaned in to speak quietly. "See? Not so terrible."

"So far." She gave him a warning look, and he had the decency to wince. "Sorry. Old habit."

"Bad habit," she corrected him as a pretty auburn-haired waitress approached them with table settings and menus. "The sooner you break it, the better off you'll be."

He rolled his eyes but didn't contradict her, so she decided to claim this round as a victory. When their table was set, she said, "Rachel McCarron, I'd like you to meet Scott Barrett, Jason's older brother."

"I've heard a lot about you," Rachel began, giving him a flirtatious grin. "Is any of it true?"

Unease flickered in his eyes, but he quickly masked it with the wry humor that had no doubt saved his sanity while he was in prison. "Probably."

When she laughed, Jenna noticed Scott didn't join in, but he wasn't exactly hiding under the table to escape the vivacious woman, either. Not that it was any of her concern, she amended silently. He was a grown man, and he could pursue whoever caught his eye. But she thought it was only fair he should know what he'd be getting into with this particular mark.

"So, Rachel," she started in a nonchalant tone. "How's that adorable daughter of yours doing thcsc days?"

Her obvious fascination with Scott wavered, and she beamed like the proud mama she was. "She's the best baby in the whole world. She'll be four months old soon. Brenda Lattimore just opened up a day care at her house, and Eva goes there while I'm working. She has a great time with all her little friends, and then I get to play with her when we get home."

"That's great," Jenna replied, pretending to skim the menu while angling a glance over at Scott. Mission accomplished, she decided when she found him gazing back at her, a knowing look in his dark eyes.

"Your family's been so great to us," Rachel continued in a gushing tone. "Especially Jason. I mean, Eva's not his daughter, so he didn't have to lift a finger to help me when I pulled into town at Christmastime. Eight months pregnant, broke and homeless," she added dramatically.

"Is that right?" he asked politely. It seemed the chatty young woman had worn him out already, and Jenna smothered a grin.

"He found me a place to live and a receptionist job that kept me off my feet. I'm telling you, that brother of yours literally saved our lives."

"He's a good guy, that's for sure."

Flashing another smile, Rachel quickly rattled off the specials, and Scott motioned for Jenna to order first. Another tick in the "gentleman" box, she thought. Maybe he was beginning to get the hang of dealing with regular people again. Based on his dustup with Alan at the hardware store, she assumed he was short on funds. In an effort to avoid cleaning out his wallet or embarrassing him if he came up short, she asked for a house salad and diet soda.

After ordering a club sandwich, he sipped his water and gave her a knowing look. "That was nice of you, but I have enough money to buy you lunch."

"I'm not that hungry, so a salad's fine."

"Before you leave town, I'll take you out for a proper dinner. Have you ever been to the Spring House over in Cambridge?"

"Are you nuts? That place is really expensive."

"Sure, but you get to work your way through the garden maze and watch the swans swimming in the pond."

It sounded as if he'd been to the antebellum mansion before, and he didn't strike her as the type to stroll around the restaurant's impeccably manicured grounds on his own. She wasn't prone to jealousy, especially over some guy she'd just met. But his exchange with Rachel was still fresh in her mind, and Jenna couldn't deny being curious about who he might have chosen to spend such a romantic evening with.

As if sensing her train of thought, he leaned his elbows on the table and grinned. "We all took Gram and Granddad there to celebrate their sixtieth anniversary. I haven't been back since."

She felt her cheeks flush and sipped her water to hide her bizarre reaction to something that was clearly none of her business. "I didn't ask."

"Yeah," he responded with a smirk. "But you were doing it pretty loudly."

She didn't have a decent comeback for that, so she opted to let it go. But she had to admit she was ridiculously pleased to discover that if they did end up having dinner together at the posh Spring House, she'd be the first woman he took there. That detail shouldn't matter even the tiniest bit to her, of course, but she was girly enough to acknowledge that it did. For some unfathomable reason, it mattered very much.

While they waited for their meal, a few people stopped at their table to chat with her and welcome Scott home. Others eyed them with curiosity but went out of their way to steer clear of them. All in all, the general opinion on Scott's return appeared to be split pretty much down the middle.

When she shared her observation, he shrugged. "Not much to be done about it. Folks're either gonna trust me or not."

"They won't just give you their trust, though," she pointed out as gently as she could. "You'll have to do things to earn it back."

"How?"

"By proving to them that you're a stand-up guy, that you're happy to be home again. Working on your family's old property is an excellent start." A slow grin was drifting across his chiseled features, and she asked, "What?"

"You think I'm a stand-up guy? Me? A bank robber?"

"The driver," she corrected him, punctuating her point with a stern glare. "Even if you'd been inside the bank with those goons, you wouldn't have stolen a dime because that's not who you are."

Leaning back in his chair, he folded his arms and studied her somberly. "What makes you so sure?"

"I know a thief when I see one." That hadn't come out the way she'd intended, and she immediately started backpedaling. "What I meant was—"

"You've seen a few thieves in your time," he interrupted, comprehension glittering in those intelligent eyes. "Why do I get the feeling you're trying really hard to not tell me something?"

"I— Well, it's complicated."

"In my experience, when someone says that, the situation's usually pretty simple. We just make it complicated to avoid telling the story 'cause it makes us angry or sad or something else we don't want to put ourselves through again. But you don't have to give me the details if you'd rather not."

She appreciated him giving her an out, and she seriously considered taking it. Then again, he'd been up-front with her about his history, so she felt compelled to do the same with him. A more subdued Rachel arrived with their meals, giving Jenna a chance to decide how to answer him.

Once they were alone, she drizzled raspberry vinaigrette on her salad and picked up the odd tale of her life where she'd purposefully left off before. "Let's see. I guess the trouble started when I quit college and was living on my own for the first time. My three roommates weren't all that picky about their friends, so I got a good look at the kind of people no one should be spending any amount of time with."

"Sounds familiar," he commented through a mouthful of Molly's homemade potato salad.

"Too familiar, I'm sure. Anyway, one

thing led to another and we ended up at the wrong party one night. I wasn't mixed up in the illegal stuff, but it didn't look good that I was there at all." The humiliation she'd felt that evening had been nothing compared to her sheer terror at being thrown in a jail cell with a dozen strangers who looked more like starving she-wolves than people. "Fortunately, when I called my foster dad, he jumped in his car right away and drove six hours in the middle of the night to bail me out. Since he was a cop, he was able to convince them to release me into his custody and let me go home with him. I didn't have a record, so his lawyer friend negotiated with the judge to get me probation and community service."

"That was the right way to handle it. Sure, you screwed up a little, but you didn't hurt anyone. At that age, you shouldn't be treated like a criminal for having bad judgment."

She'd never told anyone about this part of her past before, and while it was more than a bit unnerving, she discovered she was glad he knew the truth about her. Something told her that was important, but she wasn't quite sure what it meant to either of them. Still, she felt comfortable with everything being out in the open, so she decided it must have been all right.

"One of my community-service assignments was at this rural church that was being rebuilt after a flood. The whole congregation pitched in, doing whatever they were best at." Recalling the experience made her smile. "Imagine my surprise when I walked in that first day and found the judge from my hearing up on a ladder, stripping damaged plaster from the walls."

The irony of it made him laugh. "Didn't see that one coming, did you?"

"Not a bit." Seeing a chance to drive home a meaningful message with him, she lowered her voice and went on in a more private way. "Those people had never met me before, but they made a place for me. I'm sure the judge told them I'd had a run-in with the law, but no one ever mentioned it, just appreciated that I was there to help. When they invited me to come back for Sunday service with them, I wasn't sure. But it was nice of them to include me, and I didn't want to seem rude, so I went. It was outside in a grove of trees, and for the first time in my life I felt like I belonged somewhere."

"I'm sensing a point in there for me."

"God has a place for everyone," she reminded him gently. "We just have to step up and accept what He has to offer us."

Misery filled Scott's eyes, but he didn't look away. That alone told her how much he'd come to trust her in the short time they'd known each other. That kind of responsibility sat heavily on her shoulders, but she didn't have the heart to continue keeping him at a distance. Struggling to put his life back together, he was reaching out to her for encouragement. She simply couldn't let him down.

"There's a difference between you and me, though," he finally said, looking down as he stabbed a pickle with his fork. "You were a kid who didn't know any better. You deserved a second chance."

So that was it. All along, she'd suspected Scott hadn't drifted away from his faith out of bitterness or because he didn't care about it anymore. In fact, the opposite was true. She ached for this man who'd lost so much and had no idea how to get it back.

Reaching out, she lightly rested her hand over his, giving him space to pull away. He didn't, and when his eyes met hers again she took it as a sign that she was making progress with him. "Anyone can get another chance with God, but we have to ask Him for it."

"I don't think—"

"That's your biggest problem," she interrupted with a scowl of her own. "You think too much. If you'd just listen to your heart once in a while, you'd do better."

"I'm not an artist like you. My heart doesn't talk to me."

"Yes, it does," she informed him with a certainty that startled her. How she knew that was beyond her, but now that she'd hung the thought out there, she might as well carry it through. "But you have to listen carefully to hear what it's saying. Most folks are so busy running from one thing to another they don't stop long enough to pay attention."

That cynical look he wore so frequently was back, but as he lounged in his chair she caught a glimpse of something else, too. It was a mixture of curiosity and hope, as if he thought she might have come up with an answer for him. "What does your heart tell you?"

"All kinds of things." She stalled, searching for a coherent answer to a question no one had ever asked her. "How to capture sunlight on canvas. Which angle's best for a landscape I'm doing. How to make a gnome statue look like you could have a conversation with it," she added with a grin.

"That sounds more like talent to me. Not everyone has a gift like yours."

Any moron could figure out he was referring to himself, and she hastened to correct him. "You don't think being a good carpenter takes talent?"

"Not especially."

"I think there's a carpenter from Nazareth who might disagree with you."

Crumpling up his napkin, he tossed it on the table with a quiet chuckle. "Is this your way of trying to get me back to church?"

This guy was sharp, she had to admit. Knowing how devoted they were, she had no doubt Olivia and Diane had tried to coax him back into Pastor Griggs's fold without success. So she took another tack altogether. "Not at all. Go or don't. It's totally up to you."

"But?"

"No but," she assured him airily, tipping

her glass to spoon out a melting ice cube. "You're a big boy. You're perfectly capable of deciding that kind of thing all on your own."

He fixed her with an I'm-smarter-than-you-think-I-am grin. "But you'll be there this Sunday, right?"

"Uh-huh." Leaning toward the middle of the table, she whispered, "Don't tell anyone, but I don't sit in the rear pew 'cause I'm always late. It's because I'm a terrible singer."

He flung his head back and laughed as if she'd just told him the best joke he'd ever heard. Far from the muted, self-conscious sound she'd been able to wring out of him up until now, this one gave her a tantalizing glimpse of just how lighthearted this very serious man could be.

It only proved her theory on people in general: no matter how lost they might appear to be, there was hope for everyone. Some of them just needed a little shove to help them realize it.

Chapter Six

Thursday afternoon, Jenna arrived at the teen center, still not sure she was the right person for this assignment. She didn't have a lot of experience with kids, and she was more than a little nervous as she followed Diane through the large room where twenty or so high schoolers were spread out doing homework, clustered around the three computers or just talking.

"Gretchen?" Diane waited for her to look up and then rested a hand on Jenna's shoulder. "I'd like you to meet a friend of mine, Jenna Reed. She's the woman who owns Reed's Artworks here in town."

"Hey there," Jenna chimed in, trying to sound casual. "How's it going?"

"Pleased to meet you."

The girl's tone made it clear she wasn't the least bit pleased, and the guarded look in her hazel eyes reminded Jenna of the face that had often stared out from the mirror while she was growing up. She'd learned quickly that owning up to family problems too often resulted in well-meaning adults nosing around in things that were none of their business. Keep a calm appearance and everything was fine. But let on that you were upset and you were besieged with counselors trying to help. All that unwelcome attention only made things worse at home, so it was best to conceal your emotions. Sometimes, even from yourself.

Diane seemed to pick up on the tension and quickly said, "Well, I'll leave you girls to get acquainted. Just give a holler if you need more paper, honey."

With a brief half hug for Gretchen, she

was gone. Jenna had never taken on anything remotely like this, so she was at a loss for how to get things rolling. Thinking back to her own sullen teenage days, she pulled up a chair but sat on the other side of the table to avoid making the girl feel crowded. From her back pocket, she took out the detailed drawing she'd made of the chapel window, right down to the missing pieces. She flattened the page and studied it as if her life depended on figuring out how to finish the picture. For her part, Gretchen went right on sketching, but every now and then her eyes flicked over to Jenna.

After a few minutes of that, the girl's natural curiosity got the better of her. "What are you working on?"

Bingo, Jenna thought, smothering a proud grin. "It's kind of a puzzle, I guess." Spinning the sketch, she explained, "We found this broken window behind the wall of an old church, and I'm in charge of restoring it to the way it used to be a long time ago."

"How long?"

"Good question," Jenna approved. "That'll make a difference in what kind of glass I need and what ingredients were used to make these colors. Guess I better find out how old it is, huh?"

Gretchen shrugged as if she didn't much care, but Jenna could see she was interested. Her next question confirmed it. "Who's 'we'?"

"My friend and I." Describing Scott as a friend felt strange but right somehow. They certainly weren't enemies, and sharing some of their painful pasts had left them far more than strangers. When she realized her companion was waiting for more details, she added, "He's the carpenter in charge of rebuilding the chapel."

"So you work for him, or he works for you?"

"We work together," Jenna clarified. "Does that matter?"

"Someone's always in charge," Gretchen

replied in a way that made it sound as if she had some negative personal experience in that department. Tilting her head, she chose another shade of green pencil and continued drawing. "One person gives the orders, and everyone else follows along. That's how the world works."

To Jenna, that sounded like far too cynical an attitude for a sixteen-year-old, but that didn't mean she had it wrong. "I guess you've got a point. I like running my own business because that way I decide which projects I want to take on, how long to work and what to charge people."

"I wish I could do that," she confided with a sigh. "I hate having people tell me what to do all the time."

Jenna sensed she was starting to bend and decided to nudge a little. "Is that why you like coming here?"

"Yeah. That and the cookies," she added with a grin that hinted at a pretty good sense of humor.

"I know the lady who makes those cookies. Her name is Olivia, and I can introduce you to her sometime if you want."

Suddenly, Gretchen pulled into herself, and that protective gate slammed back into place with an almost audible clang. "That's okay. I wouldn't want to bother anyone."

This was just what Olivia needed, Jenna realized with a suddenness that startled her. So generous, with a heart full of love to share, she'd be the ideal person to encourage Gretchen without threatening her in any way. After all, who could resist a warm, loving grandmother with a plate full of cookies?

Leaning closer, she said, "Can I tell you something?"

Gretchen's eyes narrowed and she nodded hesitantly. "Okay."

"The woman I'm talking about, she lost her husband recently. She tries to pretend everything's fine, but I know she's really lonely without him. She has a great eye for art, and I know she'd really appreciate your work. If you wouldn't mind letting her hang out with you here once in a while, I think it would do her a world of good."

Folding her hands on the table, Gretchen stared at them as if debating whether to respond or not. When she finally looked up, the compassion in her eyes made Jenna want to cry. "Being lonely is hard. That's why I come to the center, 'cause the house is empty until my dad gets home at seven. I tried leaving the TV or the radio on, but it's not the same as—"

"As having your mom there?" Jenna asked gently. When the girl gulped and nodded, Jenna wanted nothing more than to fold her into a hug and tell her everything would be all right. Maybe not now, but someday. Recognizing her advice wouldn't be comforting to someone so young, she went with something more concrete. "Do you know why Diane wanted you to meet me?"

"Because you're an artist like me."

"We have more in common than that." Dredging up all this was tough for her, but she got a firm grip on her emotions and went on. "My mom left when I was your age, so I kinda get what you're going through."

Gretchen's eyes widened with the shock of finding she wasn't the only one who'd been abandoned by the woman she'd counted on to be there for her. "Didn't your dad try to find her?"

"My dad was out of the picture," she hedged, skirting the sordid truth without blatantly lying. She didn't think it was appropriate for this impressionable girl to hear the lurid details of how Jenna came to be.

"My dad's the best," Gretchen told her in a more confident tone. "He's really tired when he gets home, but he makes dinner and helps me with my homework. I do the laundry and clean the house so he doesn't have to," she added proudly.

"Good for you." Inspiration struck, and Jenna added, "Olivia's a fabulous cook.

Maybe she could teach you some of her recipes so you can surprise your father with dinner sometime."

"That would be awesome. His favorite is lemon chicken. Do you think she knows how to make that?"

"When she comes in, you can ask her. Does tomorrow work for you?"

"Sure." With a sly smile, she added, "As long as she brings some more of those chocolate-chunk cookies."

Feeling as if she'd scored the winning goal in a game that could have gone either way, Jenna laughed. "I think that can be arranged."

They sealed their deal with a high five, and Gretchen said, "That church window's probably mentioned in some dusty old book at the historical society. We could go look."

"You mean you want to help me put it back together?" Jenna asked, stunned by the quick turnaround from brooding to generous.

"Yeah. Unless you don't want me to."

"I'd love it," Jenna assured her before she could change her mind. "Maybe we can work on the actual piece together. I have a friend who makes the glass, but getting it set in place without breaking anything is tricky. I could really use an extra set of hands."

"Cool."

Very cool, Jenna thought, catching Diane's eye as Gretchen loaded up her backpack and Jenna signed them out in the logbook.

"Where are you ladies headed?" the director asked with a delighted smile.

"Over to the historical society for research," Jenna replied. "We shouldn't be more than an hour."

"Take your time," she told them. "And have fun."

"We will," Gretchen responded in an upbeat voice that would have been totally at odds with her mood only an hour ago. "Thanks, Mrs. B."

"Oh, you're welcome, sweet pea. I have

to leave early today, but I hope I'll see you tomorrow."

Grinning at Jenna, the girl nodded. "I'll be here."

While the girl headed for the door, Diane grasped Jenna's shoulders with both hands. "Bless you, Jenna. I was at my wit's end with that girl, and here you are, best friends already."

"We artistic types have to stick together," Jenna told her with a wink. "But thanks for the blessing. I'll take all of those I can get."

Feeling as if she was floating on the warm spring air, Jenna joined up with her new assistant and pointed across the street to the brick building that housed the Barrett's Mill Historical Society. Even if they found nothing in the archives about the old chapel and its mysterious window, you could always depend on Lila Donaldson for some lively company.

It would be a pleasant ending to what had turned into a very unusual day.

* * *

It had been years since Scott had been treated to a full-on Barrett family gathering.

Friday night, he met his oldest two brothers' kids for the first time and did his best to keep their names straight. Connor's boys had inherited his quick smile, while Greg's princesses doted on their toddling brother with a devotion even a curmudgeon like him could appreciate. Being referred to as "Uncle Scott" was slightly bizarre, and more than once he forgot to answer a child who called him by his new name.

Paul and Chelsea arrived on the heels of youngest brother Jason and his wife, Amy, who floated in on the bliss of a newly married couple. Their obvious happiness twanged an old nerve inside Scott, but he did his best to ignore it. Having grown up in a large, chaotic family, he'd always planned to have the same for himself one day. Going after it hadn't turned out quite the way he'd anticipated, he acknowledged for the hundredth time. Maybe, despite his longing for roots and stability, he just wasn't cut out for marriage.

Which left him on his own, at least for the foreseeable future. Being the odd one out among his brothers didn't sit well with him, but he couldn't imagine changing his bachelor status with anyone living in Barrett's Mill. And since he was stranded here until his parole played out, it wasn't looking good.

Being surrounded by all this family love only made it worse, and he felt his spirits sinking lower by the moment. It didn't help that he felt like an outsider in his own family. Being introduced to new members he already should have met was bad enough. Add to it the fact that everyone was going out of their way to include him in conversations he couldn't follow, and he finally reached his choking point.

Before someone had a chance to pick up on his morose train of thought, he made his escape to the front porch for some air. When he rested his hands on the railing, its wobbling reminded him of the first job on his list for Gram.

A little prodding revealed that the bolts holding the side rail to the column were loose. He fetched a socket wrench and pair of pliers from his truck and used them to tighten the offending bolt. While he was at it, he checked the rest and made sure they were ratcheted down nice and tight.

"You do good work. What's your hourly rate?"

He glanced up to find Jenna grinning at him and stood to greet her. Her slim white jeans and flowing top were a far cry from the paint-spattered clothes she'd been wearing the other day, and he couldn't help staring. The pale yellow blouse accentuated her eyes, deepening their icy color to a more vivid blue. As the seconds ticked by, he realized he hadn't said anything yet and managed to stammer, "Wow. You look amazing."

"Thank you."

She added a stunning smile, and crazy as it seemed, he actually felt warmer for a moment. Fortunately, it faded quickly and his brain kicked back into gear. "Glad you could make it. How was your afternoon at the center?"

"Interesting. Gretchen's a sweet girl with some big problems, but I think we made a good start toward being friends. We went over to the historical society to see if we could find the chapel window in the archives somewhere, but no luck. She seemed interested in helping me find out more about it, so we'll see how it goes."

The voice of experience, Scott mused with a frown. Things didn't always work out the way you wanted them to, and you could save yourself a lot of trouble if you kept that in mind. Since he'd exhausted his limited stock of small talk, he said, "Everyone's inside."

"Everyone but you," she noted with a

smile. "Let me guess—too much commotion for a hermit like you."

"I'm not a hermit." She tilted her head with a give-me-a-break look, and he had to laugh. "Okay, maybe a little. I'm working on it, though."

She took a step closer, and he caught a whiff of some kind of floral perfume mixed with paint thinner. It was an unusual combination, but he had to admit it suited her perfectly. When her expression sobered, he braced himself for a lecture. What he got instead was understanding.

"It must be hard to get reacquainted with your own family," she murmured. "How's it going?"

"Fine." Again he got the look, and he relented with a sigh. "Slow. I mean, I've got four sisters-in-law now. I should've danced with them at their weddings, warning them about the men they just married, y'know?"

Jenna grinned. "You strike me as the

type for a good, embarrassing toast at the reception."

"Got that right. Guess I missed my chance, though."

"You can make up for it at your own wedding," she suggested cheerily. "Everyone will love it."

"Except my wife," he pointed out, even though the words sounded weird coming from his mouth. Considering his wedding day, even in theory, just wasn't like him. Jenna had a knack for making him think about dreams he'd shut away long ago, but this time he found he didn't mind playing along. "It's probably best to behave myself and stay outta the doghouse."

"Smart man. Now, be a good host and walk me in." Taking his arm, she waited for him to open the door.

"I'm not—" He stopped short when she rolled her eyes and decided it was best to follow her lead. "Yes, ma'am."

She didn't gloat or tease him, but she

rewarded him with a bright smile that made quite an impression on his battered ego. It had been beaten so far down into the muck of his life he'd begun to fear it would never recover. But as he escorted Jenna into Gram's house, he felt himself leaning toward this talented, compassionate woman who'd done more for him in a few days than most folks could have in months of trying.

It was a good thing she wasn't planning to stay in Barrett's Mill. He might have started to rely on her in a more personal way, and that kind of thing never ended well for him.

After his earlier reaction to the crowd, he was relieved to discover he was much more comfortable with Jenna there. Probably because he actually knew her, he reasoned, and then realized that made no sense. For him, getting to know someone took a long time, and even then he was more reserved than most. Whatever the explanation, he felt better with her beside him, taking up the slack whenever he ran out of things to say.

"Jenna, none of us have seen the old homestead in years," Dad commented at one point. "How's it looking these days?"

"It's in good hands, that's for sure," she replied with a smile of approval for Scott. "Your son's got great plans for the house and the chapel. I can see why the original Barretts chose to build there. It's such a beautiful spot, set in the woods next to the creek."

"It was one of Dad's favorite places," he told her with a sad smile. "He'd be glad to know it'll be around awhile longer."

"When Scott's done with it, it'll be a great place to live again."

They both looked at him, and Scott fought down the urge to squirm like a shy kid caught in the spotlight. He didn't used to be that way, he recalled with more than a little regret. Maybe someday he'd regain the confidence that had been wired into every Barrett ever born. For now, though, it took everything he had just to keep putting one foot in front of the other.

"Thanks," he managed to say, consciously reminding himself to keep his head up when he spoke. "There's a lot still to do, but I think it's coming along."

Jenna's eyes lit with enthusiasm, and she pulled her phone from the pocket of her jeans. "Tom, I've got some pictures if you want to see them."

Dad sent a questioning look at Scott, making him stand up a bit straighter. Unaccustomed to being consulted for his opinion on things, he valued the respect his father was showing him. "There's not much to see at this point, but go ahead."

While Jenna flipped through the screens, he was surprised to see how many shots she'd taken when he hadn't been looking. One in particular caught him off guard, and he stopped her with a hand on her arm.

It showed him on the rear porch steps, turning back to say something to her before going into the house. With the lush forest and sparkling creek behind him, his hair mussed by the breeze, the man in that picture was a stranger to Scott. He looked confident and carefree, completely at home right where he was. He couldn't recall the last time he'd felt that way.

Apparently sensing his reaction, Dad rested a strong hand on his shoulder. "It's been a long time since anyone lived out at the old place, making sure things are being taken care of. I'm glad it's you."

Scott looked over at him and nearly choked on the pride shining in his father's eyes. "Thanks. That means a lot to me."

The moment gave way to a toddler tugging on Dad's hand. "Grampa, come see."

"See what, honey?"

In answer, she continued pulling, and he patted Scott's shoulder before letting her drag him to the bay window in the living room. Watching them go, Scott knew he'd let his father down—let them all down, in truth. He'd apologized more times than he could count, in emails and phone calls, but it had never felt like enough. Now, face-to-face with everyone again, the guilty burden he'd carried for so long began to lift from his heart. In its place he felt something that didn't weigh him down, but lifted him up.

Forgiveness.

The realization hit him with the force of an 18-wheeler, and he nearly staggered from the impact of it. While he'd been leery of attending this gathering, he'd agreed to come because Gram had gone to so much trouble for him and he'd wanted to return the favor. Instead, he'd gotten more than he possibly could've hoped for, regaining his place in his family. Knowing Dad had faith in him made him believe that in time, he would even feel as if he belonged here.

All because of Jenna and her camera, he mused with a grin. Go figure.

"That's a troublemaker look if ever I saw

one," Jenna teased, lightly tapping his chin. "They seem to be a Barrett-boy trait."

"Yeah, we've all got 'em, but mine's the best."

"The wickedest, anyway," she corrected with a knowing smile. "Anything you want to share with the class?"

"Just thinking you're a sneaky photographer, snapping those pictures without me noticing."

"Candids are the best," she agreed. "They show someone's personality, not just what they look like."

"Like a painting?"

That got him the most incredible smile he'd ever seen. "You were listening! Most people tune out the minute I start talking about art."

"I thought it was interesting," he told her honestly. "I'm more a hammer-and-nails kinda guy, but your stuff is pretty cool, too."

"Oh, stop," she retorted in a terrible Southern-peach accent, melodramatically fanning herself with her hand. "You're gonna turn my head."

Her antics made him laugh, and it occurred to him that he'd done that more this week than he had in ages. Bright and upbeat, this quirky artist had connected with something inside him he'd assumed was dead and gone long ago. More than anything, she'd made him believe he could stop trudging through his personal quicksand and begin enjoying life again. He had no clue how she'd accomplished that so quickly, but he hoped that before she left he'd get the chance to repay her.

While he was considering how that might work, Paul climbed up a couple steps on the main staircase and hollered for everyone's attention. Once they were all focused on him, he held out a hand and brought Chelsea up to join him. Looking out at all those expectant faces, his expression suddenly went blank, and he seemed to forget what he wanted to say. He whispered something to his wife, and she put an arm around him in a comforting gesture.

"Paul and I want you all to be the first to know we're expecting a baby in November. Before you ask, we won't know the gender, but if it's a boy, he'll be named William Henry. It's a wonderful name," she added, wrapping her other arm around Paul. "But it still makes us sad that Will won't be here to meet his new great-grandchild."

"To Granddad," Jason called out, raising his lemonade in a toast. "And another kid to buy toys for this Christmas."

They all echoed the sentiment, buzzing with questions and good wishes while they buried the happy couple in hugs and back slaps. Swept up in the tide of excitement, Scott found he shared in it wholeheartedly. Each embrace and whispered "Welcome home" bolstered his ego a little more, until he genuinely felt a part of the good things coming down the road for the Barrett clan.

Once the chaos died down, an even happier sound resonated from the kitchen: Gram's dinner bell. They all knew what that meant, and they trooped in to find the counters filled with dishes all prepared by the woman who knew everyone's favorites and made sure to include them on the menu.

When she lifted the cover off one of the roast pans, the rich aroma was enough to make Scott's stomach rumble in anticipation. She carved off a thick slice and made a show of handing it across to him, adding potatoes and carrots until he cut her off with a laugh. "Are these my leftovers, too?"

"Oh, no," she assured him with a wink. "There's another one in the fridge for you to take home with you. After you split it with Jenna, of course."

"Of course," he agreed, smiling at the guest who seemed more like a member of the family. "I'll try to be fair about it."

"Not a problem. Just remember if you stiff me, I know where you live."

Her sassy comeback made them both

laugh, and they continued their wry back-and-forth while they filled their plates and took them out to the front porch. They chatted easily while they ate, as if they'd known each other forever. Other people joined them now and then, adding their own color to the discussion before wandering off to find someone else to talk to.

It reminded him of countless picnics over the years, and Scott felt more at home by the minute. By the time he'd had his second piece of blackberry pie, he couldn't remember why he'd been so worried about this evening. It seemed silly now that he was here and having such a great time with everyone.

When he confided his impressions to Jenna, she gave him yet another understanding smile. "That's wonderful, Scott. Good for you."

"Yeah, it is, especially since restoring that old property will take me a while. I'm still not sure about the Uncle Scott thing, though. I haven't been around kids much, so it's kinda weird to think of myself that way."

After dipping her finger in whipped cream, she tapped his nose with it. "Does that help?"

Not really, he wanted to grumble, but stopped himself. Normally, he wasn't thrilled about being mocked, but the delight sparkling in her eyes nudged him to loosen up and go along with her game. Wiping off the cream, he popped his finger into his mouth and nodded. "Not bad."

"The whipped cream or me?"

She gave him a playful look that brought to mind when she'd asked something similar during their first meeting in the cemetery. This time, he answered her without a second thought. "Both."

Chapter Seven

On her way to church that Sunday, Jenna came to an intersection she'd navigated many times. One road led into town, the other out toward the sawmill and the acres of unspoiled forest that still surrounded it. Pausing, she tapped the steering wheel with her finger and debated which way to go.

She'd spent quite a bit of time with Scott this week, and she'd gotten a pretty good feel for where he was coming from. And where he wanted to go. The trouble as she saw it was that he didn't have the confidence to move beyond the longing stage and make it into his reality. Being a creative person at heart, she'd confronted obstacles all her life, both practical and personal. If you put some effort into it, you usually could find a way around the pragmatic issues. It was the personal ones that prevented you from realizing your full potential.

Looking up into the clear sky, she said, "Well, what do You think?"

Just then, a red-tailed hawk appeared overhead, banking to the west on its way to the creek for breakfast. Taking that as her answer, she cranked the wheel and headed for the old Barrett homestead. If its new owner was there, she'd take that as confirmation that what she had in mind was the right thing to do. If not, she'd try again another time. For all his rough edges, she was convinced Scott was hiding a good heart under all that bluster. If he could just bring himself to let it show, his life would be better for it.

When she pulled in, his truck was parked

in its usual spot under the oak that probably had been there since before the town existed. Remembering his warning about the front steps, she circled around back and found him sitting on the stoop, munching on a bagel. In between bites, he took a piece of crumbling concrete from the pile beside him and flung it into the creek. Judging by his lazy, steady rhythm, he'd been at it awhile.

Suddenly, her idea of dragging him to church struck her as incredibly unwise, and she hesitated. Then again, her van wasn't exactly a stealth vehicle, so he probably already knew she was here. So she gathered her courage and strolled over as if she had all the confidence in the world. "Four skips. Not bad."

"My record's seven," he told her through a mouthful of bagel. "I've been trying to match it for the last half hour."

"Seems like a nice Sunday-morning thing to do."

"Yup."

He didn't look at her, which clearly meant he wasn't thrilled to have company right now. Since she'd come this far, though, it seemed foolish to mutter a goodbye and slink away as if she'd done something wrong. Humor seemed to work best with him, so she settled on the step beside him and kept it light. "You know another nice Sunday-morning thing to do?"

His dark eyes roamed over her, and he gave her a tight smile. "Seeing as you're dressed for church, I'm thinking that's it."

"Uh-huh. What do you say?"

He finished off his breakfast in a single bite, chewing while he considered her question. That he hadn't flat-out refused was a good sign, she thought, but she'd learned that it could be hard to tell with him. He was adept at hiding everything except what he wanted her to see.

"Can I ask you a question first?" When she nodded, he went on. "Why do you care so much?"

She wasn't sure how to answer that, but the perfect response popped into her head. "Because I do. It's like the chapel, with the window sitting in between those walls, forgotten all this time. Everyone wrote that place off years ago, but I see the potential it has to be beautiful again. That's why I want to be part of bringing it back to the way it used to be."

"Yeah, I know what you mean," Scott confided in a voice filled with regret. "A lotta folks wrote me off years ago, too."

Resting her hand on his arm, she waited for him to look at her. "It's never easy to see what's beneath the surface. Fortunately for you, I have a pretty keen eye for stuff like that," she added with an encouraging smile.

He didn't respond, but gave her a long, assessing look she couldn't have read if she'd tried. Reminding herself that what he needed most from her was patience, she endured his scrutiny as graciously as she could, praying for him to come around and see her point. She might not get another chance at this, and she desperately wanted to make it work.

After what felt like forever, he patted her hand and got to his feet. "Guess I'd better go get cleaned up. Mom'd kill me if I showed up for one of Pastor Griggs's sermons looking like this."

Stunned by his decision, Jenna did her best to appear as if she'd expected him to make that choice all along. "Sounds good. Do you mind if I go poke around in the chapel a little?"

"Knock yourself out. Not literally," he amended quickly. "There's a hard hat hanging by the door. I don't trust the roof yet, so put that on before you go inside."

She really didn't think it would cave in on her, but his concern for her safety was sweet. "I will. Thanks."

"You're welcome."

He gave her a quizzical look, then shook his head and went inside the house. The man was a riddle wrapped in a maze, she thought as she crossed the overgrown yard and did a tightrope routine up the fresh stringers waiting for the new steps he obviously meant to put in. They weren't the only improvements he'd made since she'd last been here, and now she understood why he'd run out of materials.

The rotted floorboards were all gone, replaced by a run of fresh lumber that felt much more solid underfoot. The hard hat Scott had mentioned was on a nail by the door, and she smiled at the sight of order amid all the chaos. Plunking it on her head, she fastened the strap before moving farther inside to inspect his progress. The sanctuary was cozy by modern standards, and she could easily envision a small group of settlers gathering here long ago to worship together before returning to their homes for a midday meal.

The missing side windows had been replaced by boards, so she had no idea what they might have looked like. Logic suggested they would have opened up wide to allow the cooling breezes to come through during the hot Virginia summers. Not to mention the scent of honeysuckles, she thought with a smile. Back then, it must have been peaceful and pleasant in here, the ideal environment for religious services. At the rate Scott's work was progressing, by fall it would be that way again.

Sadly, she'd probably be long gone by then. She'd known that when she'd taken on the window restoration, but it hadn't bothered her to know she wouldn't see the end result. She'd been content to do her part out of respect for Will and then be on her way.

But now she felt differently about it. She wanted to see the window in its rightful place, with sunshine flowing through it into the forgotten church Scott was so determined to save. For the first time in her nomadic career, she felt her plans to leave and join the summer art season begin to waver.

"So, whattya think?"

Scott's voice broke into her brooding. When she turned to answer him, her compliment died in the back of her throat. Freshly scrubbed and dressed in navy trousers, she barely recognized him. The crisp white shirt and pale blue tie set off his dark looks perfectly, muting the dangerous vibe he carried with him. When she realized she was staring at him like a goofy teenager with a crush, she gave herself a mental shake to get her brain working again.

"I think you look respectable." Giving him another once-over, she couldn't help adding a wink. "Almost."

He laughed, and she noticed that it appeared to come more naturally to him every time he did it. "Cool. That's the effect I was going for." Glancing around, he came back to her with a raised brow. "How 'bout the chapel, though?"

This time she was ready, and she smiled.

"It looks hopeful, like the place is happy to know someone cares about it again."

Groaning, he looked at her as if she'd sprouted an extra set of arms. "Don't tell me you're one of those everything-has-a-spirit types."

"No, but this place is definitely special. It might be a wreck, but it's still God's house. Will understood that, and he was counting on you to get it, too."

Judging by his skeptical expression, Scott wasn't quite on board yet, but her faith in him was growing by the day. She had no doubt he'd get there. Eventually. Because she hated feeling chained to any kind of a schedule, she didn't wear a watch, but she sensed it was getting late. "So, are you ready to head out?"

In reply, he stepped back and motioned for her to go in front of him. Near the door, she stopped to hang the hat back on its nail. When she started to jump down, he stopped her with a hand on her shoulder. "Hang on a sec."

Swinging down, he held out his arms for her. Ordinarily, she'd refuse such a gesture on principle. Far from a helpless damsel in distress, she was a fairly athletic woman who routinely managed more difficult leaps than this one. Just as she was about to point that out to him, something made her stop.

It was his face, turned up to her expectantly, waiting for her to follow him down. He'd all but isolated himself out here on the edge of town, keeping his head down and working hard all day, every day. If it made him feel good to play the knight just this once, who was she to spoil that for him?

So she went along, and in a moment she was standing with him, his hands resting lightly on her waist. Framed by sunlight, he looked far less gloomy than he had when she'd first met him in the cemetery. When he smiled down at her, she had to fight off an admiring feminine sigh.

"Okay?" he asked. When she nodded, he backed away and began walking toward her van. "We'll have to take your van. I wasn't kidding about the truck being dead."

Just like that, their nice moment was over, and she laughed at her own foolishness. "That's fine. Do you want to drive?" she asked as he opened the driver's door.

"Your van, you drive."

While he waited for her to catch up, she marveled at how he could be so old-fashioned and modern at the same time. Other guys she'd known had felt biologically compelled to drive, no matter whose vehicle they happened to be in. Just another thing that made Scott different from, well, all of them.

It was a quick trip into town. As she turned onto Main Street, it occurred to her that he'd been all but silent on the way there. "Nervous?"

"Kinda. Folks aren't always glad to see me these days."

"Give them time," she advised while she angled into a parking spot. "Most of them will come around, and the ones that don't aren't worth losing any sleep over."

Turning to her, he met her impromptu pep talk with a muted version of his usual grin. "Thanks."

"For?"

"Not telling me how I should feel. My family means well, but they keep saying I need to keep my chin up, walk proud, stuff like that. It's not as easy as that."

"I know." Hoping to reassure him, she reached over and rubbed his shoulder. "But it'll get better."

A little boy's hope shone in those dark, pensive eyes. "Promise?"

"Promise." He stared out the windshield at the line of people going up the walk and into the Crossroads Church. Generations of his family had done the same, she realized. She couldn't imagine how awful it must be for him to believe he no longer had a place there. Before he could lose his nerve, she shook his arm. "Ready?"

"As I'll ever be. You sit in the back, right?" he asked as they left the van.

She heard the uncertainty in his voice and decided it was best to steer away from what was causing it. "Trust me, everyone else appreciates me not singing in their ears."

"What about me?"

"You're more than welcome to move if you want to. You won't hurt my feelings."

Laughing quietly, he said, "That's okay, but I'm wondering why you like singing when you're so bad at it."

"You don't have to be good at something to enjoy it," she reasoned.

"I do."

She had no trouble believing that, and she shrugged. "I guess you and I are different that way."

That got her a long, penetrating look that would have creeped her out just a few days ago. Now she understood it was his way of assessing someone, trying to decide if they deserved any more of his time. It was the same look that had freaked out Alan Pullman the other day in the hardware store, but somewhere along the line she'd gotten used to it. She wasn't sure if that was good or bad.

"We're different in a lot of ways," Scott finally murmured as they entered the sanctuary.

The personal observation was so unlike him, it caught her off guard. They took their seats on the end of the last row, and she offered him a hymnal. Hoping to keep him talking, she asked, "Really? What ways?"

"Well, there's the boy-girl thing," he replied with a wicked grin that had absolutely no business showing itself in a church.

Struggling not to laugh, she scowled at him. "That's so not funny."

Her disapproval didn't seem to faze him in the least. In fact, the grin deepened, and he leaned closer to whisper, "You can glare at me all you want, Rembrandt. Those pretty eyes of yours are smiling."

Jenna suspected that if she didn't nip this in the bud, they'd end up ruining Pastor Griggs's service for everyone around them. So she focused on the hymn board as if her life depended on memorizing the order of the songs for today.

Of course, that he'd called her by the name of her favorite artist had nothing to do with her baffling reaction to Scott Barrett. Nothing at all.

Scott hadn't expected it to be easy, coming back to church after so many years away. For once, he was right.

While everyone chatted with their neighbors, he appreciated Jenna's efforts to distract him from the sidelong glances and whispers clearly aimed in his direction. To his surprise, though, some folks offered tentative smiles, and the braver ones actually nodded at him in support. Apparently, they shared her opinion that he actually belonged here. He only wished he could say the same.

The Crossroads Church was where he'd learned his Bible verses as a child, singing "Jesus Loves Me" and embracing the faith that had sustained his family for generations. While he listened to the pastor speak about the importance of forgiveness, some of the words stuck with him longer than others, and his thoughts gradually drifted away from the sermon. It had been a long time since he'd contemplated his relationship with God, but now he couldn't seem to stop himself.

What had gone wrong? he wondered and let his memory wander back in time to when things had last felt right for him. He was stunned to realize he'd been sitting right here, trading subtle shoves with his brothers so they wouldn't get caught misbehaving. Eager to discover what lay beyond the sheltered valley where he'd grown up, he'd left not long after that and had only come back for the holidays.

In a cruel twist, the world he'd longed to explore had chewed him up and spat him out, nothing more than another country boy who'd gotten in over his head. Now here he was, struggling to reclaim the life he could've had all along if only he'd found a way to be content with what he'd had.

Jenna nudged him back to the present, and he refocused on what the pastor was saying.

"At different times in our lives, many of us find ourselves on a path that leads us into trouble." His gaze meandered through the congregation, his fatherly smile not landing on anyone in particular but somehow including them all. "Leaving that trouble behind requires us to blaze a new trail for ourselves and hopefully for others, as well. It's not easy, but our Heavenly Father is willing to give us the strength we need to make a fresh start. We need only to go to

Him with an honest, open heart and ask for His forgiveness."

Was it really that easy? Scott wondered. Now that he thought about it, after returning home he'd felt better once he apologized to his parents for letting them down. But when he looked in the mirror, the face of a guilty man still stared back at him. Maybe that was because he'd been trying to slog through this mess on his own, instead of talking to the One who could make it go away.

Lowering his head, he closed his eyes and kept it simple: *God, please help me.*

As if in response, he felt Jenna's hand on his arm and angled his head to find her watching him with worried eyes. Smiling to casc hcr concern, he realized that God had been at work already, dropping Jenna into his life just when he needed her most. Bright and cheerful, she was the ideal balance to the darkness that had been dogging him for far too long.

Reaching over, he took her hand and gave it a grateful squeeze before opening his hymnal for the final song. She hadn't exaggerated her lack of singing skills, he mused while she wandered through the notes, making a game attempt to find the right ones. Then again, when he considered her many other talents, having a tin ear wasn't so bad.

When he shared his opinion with her, she stared up at him in amazement. "Seriously? Even Amy, one of my best friends ever, can't stand it."

"I've heard worse."

Somehow, he managed to keep a straight face, but she saw right through him and laughed as a slender teenage girl and a middle-aged man approached them.

"We don't mean to intrude," the man began in a hesitant tone.

"You're not at all," Jenna assured him, boldly sticking out her hand. "You must be Gretchen's dad. I'm Jenna Reed, and this is Scott Barrett."

"Frank Lewis. It's a real pleasure to meet you both." He sounded a little more sure of himself now, and he gave Scott a friendly look. "Are you related to the Diane Barrett who runs the teen center here at the church?"

"She's my mother," he confirmed proudly.

"She's awesome," Gretchen said, eyes shining with genuine affection. "She set me up with a real-life artist so I could learn more about painting. And your grandmother's going to teach me how to cook. Isn't that cool?"

"Very cool."

Scott knew instinctively that Jenna had arranged the cooking lessons, and he silently thanked her. With Granddad gone, what Gram needed more than anything was to be involved with people, and who better than this enthusiastic girl who so obviously craved a feminine influence in her life?

Looking behind Gretchen, Jenna asked,

"Do you have something back there you want to show me?"

"I was doing some research online and found this." She brought out a wire-bound sketch pad and flipped it open to the right page. She'd printed out a photo of a stained-glass window and taped it to the paper.

"That's our window," Scott blurted in surprise. "Where'd you find it?"

"Well, Jenna said your family built the chapel, so I checked out your history on one of those genealogy websites. The Barretts who settled here were originally from Wales," she informed him proudly. "Did you know that?"

He did, but he hated to dampen her enthusiasm, so he played dumb. "Huh. How 'bout that?"

"Anyway, there's a pretty church in their hometown, and the altar window looks a lot like the one here." Turning to Jenna, she added, "The Welsh one isn't missing any pieces, so I was thinking you could use it as a model for the one you're restoring."

"The one *we're* restoring," Jenna corrected her, hugging her around the shoulders. "So far, you've done all the work. Are you up to finishing the job?"

"Totally," she gasped, joy lighting her eyes. "It would be fabulous to keep working with you."

"Not so fast," Jenna cautioned sternly. "A freelancer never agrees to anything until she knows how much it pays."

"You're gonna pay me?" When Jenna nodded, Gretchen looked as if she was ready to explode. "How much?"

Jenna named a reasonable number, then shifted her focus to the girl's father. "As long as you think that's appropriate, of course."

"More than," he agreed instantly. The gratitude that flooded his gaunt face made it clear the money would be very welcome in their family. Folding her hand in both of his, he gently shook it. "God bless you, Miss Reed."

"He already has," she assured him. "And it's Jenna. One condition on this gig, though." Pinning her assistant with a deadly serious look, she said, "School comes first. Before you come to my studio, all your homework has to be done. If your grades start slipping, the deal's off. Got it?"

Nodding eagerly, Gretchen launched herself at Jenna for a ferocious hug, and Scott heard her whisper, "You're the best."

Funny, Scott thought as the Lewises headed for the door. He knew exactly how Gretchen felt.

His family was coming down the aisle, and he braced himself for some fussing about him attending the service. To his great relief, no one mentioned it, and they all walked out as if they went to church together every Sunday morning.

When they were out front, Paul caught him by the arm. "Are you busy?"

"As a one-armed paper hanger." It was one of their father's favorite comebacks, and they both laughed. "What'd you need?"

"Think you could come over and take a look at our dining room?" Chelsea was talking with Jenna, and Paul slid a look her way before leaning in to mutter, "She's worried about you getting the breakfront for our dining room done before the baby's born."

"That's what you get for marrying an accountant," Scott teased, getting a tight frown in reply. Suddenly concerned, he asked if everything was okay.

"Never better."

He added a smile, but Scott had known this guy all his life. His lighthearted big brother was worried about something, and judging by the faint shadows under his eyes, it had nothing to do with the furniture business. Narrowing his eyes, he said, "That might work on the rest of the family, but this is me you're talking to. Spill it."

"Not here," he stalled, glancing at the

people milling around, chatting and laughing. "Come to the house, and I'll fill you in."

"I drove in with Jenna. That old truck's giving me fits."

"Actually, that's perfect. She can keep Chelsea occupied while we talk."

The relief in his brother's voice was impossible to miss. Apparently, he needed someone to confide in, and Scott was elected. How that had happened, he wasn't sure, but he suspected it was because whatever Paul had to say would freak out their parents, and Jason was too caught up in being a newlywed to be much good in a crisis.

It had been a while since someone had needed him for anything important, but to his surprise, Scott was glad to be chosen. He wasn't sure how much help he'd actually be, but at least he could listen. When Jenna and Chelsea joined them, he asked, "Jenna, would you mind going over to their house for a little while? I want to look at their woodwork and take some measurements for Chelsea's new buffet."

"No problem," she replied immediately, smiling at the parents-to-be. "I was planning to do a fairy-tale mural in the nursery as a shower gift. This way, I can get an idea how big it should be and what colors to use."

"Oh, that's wonderful!" Chelsea exclaimed with a quick hug. "Thank you for thinking of it."

"It suits me well, too," Jenna commented with a wink. "I won't have to ship a gift to you from wherever I am."

They all started walking, and somehow the girls wound up sandwiched between Paul and Scott. The cozy arrangement should've felt strange to him, but for some reason it didn't. Why, he couldn't exactly say, but it didn't take a genius to figure out his new perspective had a lot to do with the sunny, sweet-tempered artist he'd been hanging out with lately.

"I wish you didn't have to go," Chelsea

was saying in a wistful tone. "Amy and I are really gonna miss you."

"I'll miss you guys, too, but I take in more than half my money for the whole year during the summer art circuit. Without that, I might have to break down and get a real job," she added with a convincing shudder.

"I know what you mean," Chelsea answered as they headed across the town square to the stately old colonial she and Paul were rehabbing. "Once I started working at the mill with Paul, doing all kinds of different, interesting things every day, I couldn't stand the thought of going back to the bank."

They'd all grown up together, and Scott remembered Chelsea being a quiet bookworm who didn't have time for much beyond studying and more studying. How she'd blossomed into this vibrant, caring woman was a mystery to him. It just proved that under the right circumstances anyone could change. Another lesson for the troubled man in his mirror, he realized.

When they reached the front door, Paul turned to face them with a grim expression. "Calling this house a work in progress is a huge understatement. Just wanna warn you."

"I had to move my bed from under a new leak in the roof last night," Scott told him with a chuckle. "How bad can this place be?"

That seemed to ease Paul's mind, and he unlocked the door to let them inside. The walls were plain Sheetrock, and a couple of them sported various swipes of paint. The colors weren't even remotely similar, and Scott assumed that meant his brother and sister-in-law were having a tough time agreeing on—well, everything.

"Come on upstairs," Chelsea said to Jenna. "The nursery's in good shape, so you can get an idea of where your mural will look best."

"You and Paul are going to make such wonderful parents," Jenna commented, smiling over at him. "You must be so excited about the baby."

"A little terrified, too," Chelsea confided with a hesitant expression. "Being a mom is such a huge responsibility."

"Oh, you'll do fine," Jenna told her. "You've had lots of practice the last few months with the crew out at the mill. Not to mention Paul and Jason."

"You're hilarious," Paul growled good-naturedly and then said to Scott, "Are you sure you want her helping out at your place? She can be a real pain."

"Really?" Grinning at her, he added, "Guess we have something in common, after all."

As she and Chelsea headed upstairs, Jenna turned back and actually stuck her tongue out at him. Much as he hated to admit it, he really liked her spunk. She took things in stride that upended most folks, and she viewed the world with a cheerful disposition he wouldn't mind sharing.

Paul watched them go with worried eyes, and Scott put aside his musings to focus on more serious things. Once the girls were out of earshot on the second floor, Scott took a seat on an antique piano stool in the living room. He noticed there was no piano, but decided not to irritate his brother by mentioning it. "What's up?"

"It's the mill," Paul confessed with a sigh. "We were hoping to be further into the black by now, but it's not looking all that promising."

From memory, he rattled off a hefty list of problems with suppliers and spreadsheets, and Scott could hardly believe what he was hearing. Paul had always been the easygoing one, good at everything he tried the first time around. When he finished his sad story, Scott finally grinned. "You sound like a businessman."

"Wish I felt more like one," he grumbled with a scowl.

"The obvious solution is to add another product or two to the catalog for your customers. Any thoughts?"

By the way he was eyeballing Scott, it was clear Paul already had come up with an idea and was using this little powwow to test the waters. Realizing he'd been set up, Scott swallowed a groan. "Okay, hit me."

"Affordable custom cabinetry is big these days. Folks send you their dimensions, you design and build the cabinets for them or their contractor to install. It could be just the thing to get us over this hump and stabilize the mill's cash flow."

"Which lets Chelsea take some time off without worrying too much about keeping up with the books," Scott commented to show he understood there was more to this problem than money.

"Yeah. The problem is, we don't know if it'll fly or not. That's where you come in," he added with one of those big-brother grins Scott used to hate. Paul hauled them out when he was trying to talk Scott or Jason into doing something against their better judgment. The fact that he usually suc-ceeded said as much about them as him, Scott recalled with a grimace.

Then again, Barrett's Sawmill had failed once before during its long history. If he was capable of helping Paul avoid a repeat per-formance, he'd do what he could. "What've you got in mind?"

"You do great work, and if we can show people that, we can gauge how much in-terest there might be in this kind of thing. You make a few pieces, we put 'em up on the website and see what happens. It could solve all our problems."

Or create a bunch of new ones. Scott forced the negative thought back down where it belonged. He was trying desper-ately to move on with his life. He'd never get anywhere if he kept viewing every opportunity from the bleakest angle possible.

"Okay, I'm in. Since I promised Chelsea this buffet anyway, why don't I start with that?"

"Great idea," Paul approved with a broad grin. "It'll make her happy twice, and make me look like a genius."

"Yeah, that's what I live for." He figured there was no time like the present, so he pushed himself to his feet and looked through the unfinished arch into the dining room. "Why don't you show me what you've got in mind? I'll grab some measurements and draw up a few concepts for you guys to look at so I can put together a materials list and get started on the build."

"And after that's done?"

Unaccustomed to considering anyone else in his plans, taking on this challenge was a real stretch for him. As Paul eagerly waited for his answer, Scott hunted for other options and came up with exactly none. It was

him or nothing, apparently, and he relented
with a sigh. "I'll get the cabinetry line going
so you can see how it'll work. If you decide
to follow through with it, you're gonna need
to hire someone for real."

"Will do."

Slinging an arm around Scott's shoulders, Paul walked him into the bare dining room and pointed out the hand-carved
crown molding and trim framing the doors
and windows. While Scott listened, he got
the distinct impression that Paul believed
he'd corralled a permanent cabinetmaker
for the Barrett's Sawmill brand.

Scott had no intention of staying in town
any longer than legally necessary, but he
didn't have the heart to tell his brother that.
So, in the interest of family harmony, he
kept his mouth shut.

Chapter Eight

As an artist there was nothing Jenna adored more than sinking everything she had into a project and giving her creative spirit free rein over the rest of her life. Sometimes she got so engrossed in what she was doing, she even forgot to eat. Then she'd look up and realize the sun had gone down and most of the day had spun around her without her noticing the passing hours.

Standing in her darkening studio on a cloudy Wednesday afternoon, she folded her arms and stepped back from the wall to assess the progress of the piece she was sketching onto a large piece of see-through paper. This one wasn't exactly work, of course. It was a labor of love for the new little Barrett who would be coming into the world soon.

A child she wouldn't get a chance to meet, she acknowledged with a frown. The large, raucous family that had given this charming town its name and iconic sawmill had embraced her from her first days here, making her feel at home. In all her years of wandering, that had never happened to her, and she couldn't deny it was making her question her commitment to the traveling art circuit that would begin in a few short weeks.

Every summer, she'd happily packed her artwork and everything she owned into her van, taking off on her latest adventure. Reconnecting with old friends at the fairs, making new ones, exploring different places—those had always been her favorite elements of the life she led. Long before it was time to leave wherever she was, she

looked forward to shedding her more settled existence and embracing the freedom
of life on the road.

Except this year.

Glancing over at the large calendar she
used to keep track of her projects, her eyes
went to the six-month outlook spread across
the bottom. In a few days, she'd be crossing off April and ticking off the few remaining commissions that would take her
through Memorial Day. Her final obliga-
tions were the chapel window and Chelsea's
shower gift. After that she'd head out to join
a weeklong art show in Georgia.

Normally, the very notion of it would fill
her with excitement. This time, she was
having mixed feelings, which was almost
unheard of for her. Because she ran her own
business, she had to be reasonable about
what she took on. She couldn't follow every
whim, but on the flip side, she refused to
spoil her fun by overthinking things. When
there was a decision to be made, she tried

to be sensible, but in the end her heart ruled the day.

Unfortunately, today her heart was leading her in an unfamiliar—and kind of scary— direction. For the first time she could recall, she found herself seriously considering renewing her lease and staying put for another year. The more she thought about it, the better it sounded to her, and she stared out the window, trying to pinpoint what might have caused this unexpected change.

While she was pondering, she heard a now-familiar engine out on the road and watched as Scott's ancient truck pulled around the curve and into the circular drive in front of her studio. When he climbed from the cab, her heart did a little flip that made her sigh in resignation. He might not be the entire reason for her wanting to stay, but she couldn't deny he was a big part of it.

Instinct warned her he wouldn't be at all pleased to know that, so she buried that strange feeling down deep and went to greet him at the door. "This is a nice surprise. What brings you by?"

"Nothing in particular," he hedged warily. "Just wanted to say hi."

He looked like a stray ready to bolt, and she felt her attraction to him getting stronger. Hiding behind that stoic demeanor was a great guy, and she wished he'd drop his guard long enough to let other people see that side of him. Since she didn't want to spook him with such a personal observation, she gave him her brightest smile. "Hi."

Slowly, his somber look gave way to one of those knee-weakening grins. "Y'know, you've got the best smile. It's like sunshine."

Guys complimented her all the time, and she normally took remarks such as that in stride. But coming from Scott, the comment really meant something. "That's sweet of you to say."

"You sound surprised."

"I am," she admitted with a laugh. "Up to

now, I had the impression you were more the grumbly-bear type."

"Well, you caught me on a good day."

"I'm glad. You haven't had many of those since you came back."

"Tell me about it."

His weary tone suggested to Jenna that he wanted to chat, so she led him to the pair of lawn chairs and flea-market table in what she called her take-a-break corner. Opening the little fridge to get herself a bottle of water, she asked, "Do you want something?"

He dipped his head to look inside. "Sweet tea would be nice. Thanks."

After handing a bottle to him, she looked up and found him studying her with a curious expression. She'd grown accustomed to his dark, intense gaze, so this lighter one threw her a little. "What?"

"You always seem to know what I need even before I do," he answered, lifting his drink as proof of what he was saying. "How do you manage that?"

"After my scrape with the law, I figured it would be smart to learn how to read people better," she explained as they sat down. "I did some research on psychology and behavior, stuff like that."

"Kinda like profiling?"

"I guess." Taking a sip of water, she continued, "The main idea is to listen more than you talk, and pay as much attention to how people act as you do to what they say. Once you learn how to interpret those clues, you can tell when someone's for real and when they're trying to put one over on you."

Clasping his bottle between his hands, he leaned forward and rested his elbows on his knees. Admiration glittered in his eyes, drawing her a little closer to this handsome, bewildering man who'd intrigued her from the moment she'd met him. "So do you think I'm for real?"

Trapped by the intensity of that stare, at

first she could only nod. His gaze warmed with something she couldn't begin to define, and she feared she was losing her battle to keep herself at a safe distance. It would be so easy to fall for this guy, with his sharp wit and quick mind. The problem was, she didn't think either of them was ready for anything serious right now.

In spite of that, she couldn't bring herself to tell him anything other than the absolute truth. "You're one of the most real people I've ever met. Even when you know folks won't like what you have to say, you're honest with them. That takes a lot of courage, and I admire that about you."

A smile quivered at the corner of his mouth. "That's interesting, 'cause I feel the same way about you."

"Really?" Beyond flattering, it was a judgment on the kind of human being she was. Most guys didn't look beneath the surface to discover there was any more to her than what they saw at first glance. That only made Scott more appealing than he already was, and she fought down emotions she'd never had to work all that hard to control. "That's nice to hear."

For some reason that made him laugh, and she scowled at him. "What's so funny?"

"You. Did you know when you're uncomfortable with something you scrunch up your nose like a rabbit?"

The urge to rub her nose was almost irresistible, but she managed to resist the impulse. "I do?"

"Never go up against a real gambler, Rembrandt," he cautioned as he stood and set his empty bottle on the table. "You'll lose every time."

With that, he flashed her another maddening grin and sauntered back out the way he'd come in. Based on his less-than-stellar past, his advice didn't surprise her in the least. Finding that he'd picked up on something about her behavior that no one else had ever mentioned didn't, either.

Having such a private man share his impressions of her, however, was downright astounding. While she watched his truck drive away, she was fairly certain something very important had just taken place between them.

But she couldn't figure out what on earth it was.

Later that night, Scott lay awake, listening to the rain and staring at the ceiling. At first, he told himself he was just making sure the patch he'd installed on the roof was holding up. But as the hands on the old manual alarm clock on his bed stand moved past midnight, he finally had to admit the truth.

Jenna Reed had gotten to him.

The more time he spent with the free-spirited artist, the more he liked her. She was fun and engaging, with a caring heart to balance out her amazing looks. God knew what He was doing when He put her together, Scott acknowledged with a grin.

And maneuvering them onto intersecting paths? Divine genius.

So what was he going to do about it? Dropping by her studio today had proven to him that how he felt about her when she wasn't around only intensified when they were together. Even his sharp memory couldn't do her justice, and he kept catching himself inventing reasons to be with her. She wouldn't be around much longer, and if he wanted her to leave town with a lasting memory of him, he'd have to do something soon.

Maybe, if things went well between them, she'd swing back through the Blue Ridge Mountains on her summer tour. The trouble was, with his track record it was entirely possible he'd go out on that limb and make a complete fool of himself. The idea of such a personal failure didn't bother him all that much. Every relationship he'd ever gone into had ended badly—none worse than the last one. But he'd survived all that and had come out the other side wiser than he'd gone in.

While his brain wasn't sure he was ready to take that plunge again, Jenna had managed to find a way into parts of him he'd closed off years ago. It was his heart that was keeping him awake tonight, he realized. Pummeling him with images of her until he couldn't do anything other than accept that they were real and weren't likely to fade anytime soon.

He'd seen the same sentiment reflected in her eyes earlier when she looked at him with admiration and declared him to be an honest person. The incredible thing was when she said it he believed her. Not only that she meant it, but that it was true. Knowing her history and how hard she'd worked to avoid making the same dangerous mistakes again, he trusted her judgment about him.

More than that, he realized, she had confidence in him. In his ability to make a new life here, to reconnect with the faith he'd lost. Most of all, she believed he could be happy again. Everything she'd done since their unexpected meeting—from offering to help with the chapel to running interference at the hardware store—had been aimed at helping him overcome his faulty past and take on a brighter, more promising outlook.

Closing his eyes, he listened to raindrops drumming on the roof, sifting through the leafy branches outside his window to splash down in puddles on the ground. The sounds had a hypnotizing effect, and as he began to drift off his last thought of the day made him smile.

Despite the obvious challenges, he wanted his future to include Jenna. It wouldn't be easy, but he was a Barrett. Somehow he'd figure out a way to make it happen.

Jenna was touching up the frosted sign on the glass door of Arabesque when Amy, the shop's owner, appeared on the other side. She held up a mug with a questioning look, and Jenna motioned for her to wait a second. When she'd finished the points on the ballet dancer's toe shoes, she nodded and Amy pushed the door open to join her out front. A former ballerina herself, the town's dance teacher was tiny but a force to be reckoned with. Something her lumberjack husband would be the first to admit.

"Oh, that's much better," Amy approved heartily. "The sunlight really does a number on that poor dancer."

"I tried a different paint formula this time," Jenna replied, taking a sip of a rich, aromatic blend of caffeine and vanilla. "Hopefully, that'll help the design last longer."

Her friend's cheerful look disintegrated. "So you're really not coming back in the fall?"

"Backtracking is never part of my plan, Amy," Jenna reminded her as gently as she could. "You know that."

"Plans change sometimes. I never thought I'd find someone like Jason and settle down anywhere other than New York City, but it ended up working out perfectly for me."

"I wish I had whatever gene makes people happy to be rooted in one place for years at a time," Jenna confided with a sigh. "For some reason, God made me a wanderer."

"You could live here," Amy suggested hopefully, "and travel to the different shows over the summer. There are plenty of them around where you could sell your pieces."

"That's not how I do things." Even to her own ears, it sounded like a lame excuse, and she tried to explain her reasoning more clearly. "I've learned it's better to leave a month too soon than stick around a month too long. I know it's hard to understand, but you have to trust me on this one. It's best for everyone."

"What about Scott?" Amy sipped her fragrant tea with a casual air, but when she looked up, Jenna got the distinct impression there was something devious spinning around in Amy's mind.

Figuring two could play that game, she shrugged. "What about him?"

"It seems to me like you two are getting along really well. Everyone else thinks so, too."

So that was it, Jenna realized with a grin. The Barrett's Mill gossip mavens had declared Scott and her an item. Much as she hated having people stick their noses into her personal business, she had to admit this particular intrusion was kind of sweet. The ladies around town thought the Barretts' prodigal son needed a special woman in his life, and they'd chosen her.

The scary thing was, the more she rolled the idea around in her head, the more it appealed to her. Scott was definitely more pragmatic than she was, but the cynicism he'd worn like a shield had gradually faded as he'd gotten accustomed to being home. It had left behind a sharp wit she enjoyed immensely. Because he had a creative bent of his own, he understood her passion for art, listening intently whenever she talked about her latest project.

Somehow, when she wasn't looking, their friendship had started growing into something more. His impromptu visit the other evening popped into her mind, and she wondered if there had been more to it than mere boredom.

"Earth to Jenna," Amy said with a quiet laugh. "Did I lose you?"

"Sorry. What were you saying?"

"I was asking about the mural you're doing for my future godchild. How's it coming along?"

"Fine. I think," she added with a grimace. Then inspiration struck, and she said, "Actually, if you've got time, I could use your help."

"Me?" Amy laughed, quieting when she seemed to realize Jenna was serious. "What on earth for?"

"I've got some dancing animals in the forest, and the sketches just don't look right to me. I was hoping you could go over to the nursery with me and give me some motion perspective so I can picture the scene better."

"Umm…okay." Clearly hesitant, she went on. "I'm not sure what you mean by that."

"It's hard to describe. It might make more sense when you see it."

"I'll give it a shot," she agreed, taking Jenna's empty mug from her. "I'm done with classes for today, so we can do it now if you want."

"Perfect. Thanks."

After a quick call to make sure Chelsea was up for company, Amy went inside for her key and flipped the window sign to read Back Soon. Jenna grabbed her rolled-up sketch from the van, and they walked down the sidewalk toward the center of town. It was a beautiful Saturday afternoon, with a warm breeze swirling in one moment and retreating the next. The effect was almost playful, and by the smiles and laughter she heard from shoppers and diners on Main Street, the effect was contagious.

Such a pretty town, she thought for the countless time. From its centuries-old oaks to the solemn granite war memorial in the park, Barrett's Mill had a timeless quality to it. The charming old buildings and quaint churches only added to the image, and she knew that no matter where else she traveled in her life, this town would always have a special place in her memories.

When they arrived at Paul and Chelsea's, Jenna was surprised to see three familiar pickups lined up in the turnaround next to Chelsea's classy silver convertible. Even before she knocked, she heard male voices inside debating something so important it was worth shouting about.

"They can't hear us knocking," Amy suggested with a smirk. "You think they'll notice us if we just walk in?"

"Only one way to find out."

Pushing open the heavy oak-paneled door, she strode in to find three of the infamous Barrett brothers mired in a standoff in the center of the dining room. Chelsea stood near a window, arms folded, apparently waiting for them to run out of air. When she saw Amy and Jenna, her dour expression brightened immediately, and she waved them over.

"Ridiculous, aren't they?" she asked, shaking her head.

"What on earth are they arguing about?" Amy demanded with a scowl.

"Wainscoting."

Chelsea had a great sense of humor, and Jenna waited for her to laugh and fill them in on the real issue, but she didn't.

"You've got to be kidding me," Jenna scoffed. "Doing wainscoting means you panel half the wall and trim it out, right?"

"Right."

"Then what's the problem?"

"How big the squares are supposed to be," Chelsea explained in an exasperated tone. "It seems there are different ways to do it, and they all have their own idea on which is best."

After about ten seconds of listening to them spit and bluster at each other, Jenna had had enough. They were much taller and stronger than she was, but that had never stopped her before. Wading into the thick of things, she pushed them apart and glowered at each of them in turn.

"Problem, boys?" When they all started to answer, she stopped them with her hands in the air. "One at a time. Paul?"

"Oh, sure," Jason sulked. "Ask the oldest."

"Since it's his house, I'm starting with him. You'll get a turn. As long as you don't make me any madder," she added sternly.

He rolled his eyes but clamped his big mouth shut. Figuring that was the best she'd get from him, she eyed Scott for his reaction.

"Don't look at me," he said defensively. "I don't care how big the panels are, as long as I only have to cut 'em once. This reclaimed oak's over a hundred years old, and I don't wanna waste any of it."

Leave it to Scott to view the situation from its most practical angle. Finally, she was making some progress. When Paul gave pretty much the same explanation Chelsea had, Jenna took a moment to assess the large room. Anyone with eyes could see the walls weren't true, and it wouldn't surprise her a bit to learn that the measurements differed from one section to the next. A solution popped into her head, and she sent up a silent prayer of gratitude.

"Okay, I see what's going on here. You guys need some perspective."

"I'll say," Amy muttered, glaring at her husband.

"Not that kind," Jenna corrected her with a laugh. "I mean you've got an oddly shaped room with lots of windows and this huge arched doorway. If you try to measure it and then split the wall space up evenly, it might be correct, but it'll look weird."

She had their attention now, and she picked up a pencil to draw while she described her suggestion for addressing their dilemma. In a nutshell, it amounted to custom-fitting each piece, adjusting the dimensions as they went. That way, the human eye would see straight lines, even if technically there weren't any. When she was finished, she looked around the masculine circle and was thrilled to find them all nodding.

"Makes sense to me," Jason said first and then glanced over at Chelsea. "Sorry for getting so loud. We're just trying to make it perfect for you guys."

"I know. But in the interests of family peace and quiet—" she nailed Paul with a disapproving look "—I think Jenna's idea is the best approach."

"Just out of curiosity," Scott began, glancing from Amy to Jenna. "What are you two doing here?"

"Girl stuff," Chelsea informed him primly, turning on her heel to head toward the stairs. "We have a lot to talk about, so keep it down or I'll call your mother."

Upstairs in the nursery, Chelsea turned to her guests with a sigh. "It's been like that all morning. I love them, but sometimes…"

"Bullheaded Barretts," Amy groused with an indulgent smile that gave away her true feelings. "Gotta love 'em."

"Or not," Jenna piped up, making them all laugh.

"So, what do you need?" Chelsea asked as they crossed the room to where the mural was half sketch and half misty painting.

Studying it to refresh her memory, she tapped her chin and frowned. "These dancing animals look stiff to me."

"They're two-dimensional," Amy reminded her. "There's not much you can do about that."

"Maybe not, but I want them to look more like the ballerina at Arabesque. Amy posed for that to give me a starting point, and I think that might work here, too. If you two could help me out, I'll give it another go."

They eagerly agreed, and she let each of them find a comfortable dancing position they could hold for a few minutes while she fixed her drawing. Inspired, she dug in her front pockets and found several pieces of chalk left over from the terra-cotta pot she'd been working on that morning.

Moving quickly, she shaded in the green grass and leaves, then added some brown and blue, accenting everything with a peachy color she blended with her fingertips. Later, she'd go over them with paint, but for now it was a huge improvement. When she stepped back, she couldn't keep back a smile. "Much better."

"It's beautiful," Chelsea breathed, slowly shaking her head. "I've never watched you work, and now that I have I'm even more impressed by how talented you are."

Jenna's cheeks warmed, and she averted

her eyes while she jammed the chalk back into her overalls. "Thanks."

"Have you ever thought about displaying your art in a gallery somewhere?" Amy asked. "There's one in Roanoke, and I'm sure they'd love what you do."

"Maybe," she hedged. When they eyed her curiously, she gave in with a laugh. "Okay, you caught me. It's a dream of mine to be featured in an actual gallery someday. The problem is, they have to be able to sell what I bring them. That means I'd have to give them what their clients are looking for, and that means—"

"You'd have to play by the rules," Chelsea finished with an understanding smile. "I hear you. It's a lot more fun to do things on your own terms than follow someone else's agenda."

"I still think you could have it both ways," Amy insisted, her dancer's soul shining in her eyes. "There's nothing more amazing than sharing your gifts with people who can truly appreciate them."

"Maybe," Jenna repeated. "But for now, I'm happy to have this—" she tapped the evolving mural "—figured out. Now that I'm not stuck, it should be done next week."

One more project down, she thought. One day closer to leaving. It seemed that as her time here continued to dwindle, the more she doubted it was the right way for her to go. Pushing her predicament aside, she focused on what Chelsea was saying.

"—would love to have you stay for dinner. Paul's trying out his new grill, and I think he bought enough meat for half the town. He also said something about finishing the horseshoe pit out back, so it could be pretty entertaining watching the boys try to outdo each other."

"Count us in," Amy chimed in immediately. "After all that nonsense earlier, the guys can make it up to us by taking care of dinner."

They all laughed, and as they made their way downstairs, Jenna felt something she couldn't quite identify at first. When they reconnected with the guys, though, it hit her with a certainty that made her question why she hadn't seen it before.

She belonged here.

With these warm, engaging women and the funny, aggravating men who'd nearly come to blows over a woodworking project. When Scott glanced up from the piece of trim he was measuring and grinned at her, she felt a sudden rush of emotions so strong she actually lost her breath.

His jaw tensed, and he hurried over to where she was trying to regain her balance. "You okay?"

"Fine," she managed to answer more or less normally. "Why?"

"You just went white as a sheet, that's why. Come on, let's get you some fresh air."

She wasn't usually prone to any kind of spells, but this one was a doozy. Bewildered by what was happening to her, Jenna allowed him to lead her onto the front porch and guide her to sit on the top step.

Settling in beside her, he studied her with dark, anxious eyes. "You want some water?"

"No, I'll be okay. I guess it was all the dust you guys are kicking up in there." She offered up a weak smile that clearly didn't fool him for a second.

"You work with plaster and ceramics every day," he said bluntly. "You're used to a little dust."

"The heat, then." What was wrong with her? She detested women who behaved like hothouse orchids that couldn't bear up under the slightest strain. Giving herself a mental shake, she forced a more convincing smile. "Whatever it was, I'm over it. Sorry to worry you."

"You're sure?" When she nodded, he gave her a long, dubious look. "Okay, but I'm gonna keep an eye on you. If you start getting pale like that again, I'm taking you to a doctor."

"Okay."

Suddenly tired beyond words, she rested her head on his strong shoulder and closed her eyes. Without a word, he put his arm around her in a protective gesture that made her heart sigh in contentment.

For so long, she'd relied only on herself, terrified of creating the kind of bond that had the potential to break her heart. Somehow, when she hadn't been paying attention, Scott had come to mean much more to her than he should have. Even now, cuddled against him on this sunny afternoon, she knew she should politely disentangle herself and go home.

But she didn't.

"Are you gonna finish that?" Jason asked, pointing his fork at the small hunk of sausage left on Scott's plate.

"Knock yourself out." Stuffed to the gills

with grilled chicken, sausage and peppers, he leaned back in his lawn chair and tipped his head back with a sigh. "Hope y'all don't mind having me for company tonight, 'cause I can't move."

"Anyone who stays has to help me finish up that wainscoting," Paul told him, probably only half-joking.

"Whatever."

The afternoon had rolled on into a leisurely evening in Paul and Chelsea's backyard, testing a variety of meats and vegetables on the grill, putting away gallons of sweet tea, talking and laughing about nothing in particular. The breeze swept through once in a while, rustling the branches overhead and picking up the scents and sounds of other folks enjoying their own barbecues.

Serene but fun, it brought to mind those long-ago summer nights when he'd been growing up in this tiny, close-knit community that managed to defy the modern world and remain the same year after year.

When he was younger, he'd considered that a drawback to life in Barrett's Mill. Now, like the creek that ran behind his house, it was comforting in a way he never would have anticipated as an eighteen-year-old eager to explore the country.

Jenna being there with him had a lot to do with his contentment, he recognized. Lolling his head to the side, he watched her chatting with Amy, both of them animated and laughing at something he suspected wouldn't make a lick of sense to him. Much as he liked his own company these days, he couldn't deny that Jenna's bright energy was like a beacon for him, lighting his way back to the trail he'd abandoned years ago.

It might not be as exciting as traveling wherever his imagination took him, but that didn't mean it was bad. Since leaving his very traditional roots, right and wrong gradually had become so murky for him, he'd lost his ability to tell the difference between them. Without being preachy, Jenna had reminded him, helping him correct his course to one he could be proud of.

No matter what happened between them, he'd always be grateful to her for that. He only hoped that before she left, he'd be able to come up with a way to thank her properly for all she'd done.

Scott's meandering thoughts came to a sudden halt when a huge burgundy truck turned in from Ingram Street and parked behind the other cars in the driveway. With flames painted along both sides and tires taller than most men, it looked like an escapee from the monster-truck expo. Letting out a whistle, he said, "Nice wheels. Whose truck is that?"

No one answered, but his brothers traded a look that told him they'd cooked this up together. Never a good sign. "Aw, come on," he groaned. "You know how much I hate surprises."

"Not this one," Paul commented with a grin.

Scott glanced over again and actually blinked in disbelief as he slowly got to his feet. After climbing down, the tall, long-legged driver striding toward them grinned and made a beeline for where he stood. "How you been, Scotty?"

"Heath?" The two embraced warmly, and he asked, "Last I heard, you were dangling off an oil rig in Alaska somewhere. What're you doing here?"

"Same thing you boys are, apparently," he replied easily, greeting everyone with a quick wave. "Eating Paul outta house and home. Plus, I heard something about horse-shoes. Do you boys throw 'em the hard way, or do you still take 'em off the horse first?"

Chuckling at that, Paul offered a hand and then turned to his wife. "You remember Heath Weatherby, don't you?"

"Vividly," she replied with a laugh of her own and then hugged him. "Welcome home."

"Thanks." Turning to Amy, he said, "Your

uncle wanted me to tell you the new alternator he ordered for your car came in today. I'll install it on Monday and drop the car off at your place. If you have any more problems, just let me know."

"That works. Thanks so much."

"Anytime."

When Scott noticed Jenna eyeballing their guest, he remembered his manners and introduced her. "Heath, this is Jenna Reed, our resident artist."

"Nice to meet you." Giving her a quick once-over, he added an approving male grin. "I'm no expert, but I'd say you make this town pretty enough just by walking around."

"Down, boy," Scott grumbled, pushing him onto a bench with a little more force than was strictly necessary. They'd been friends since birth, and Heath gave Scott a wink of understanding that irritated him for some reason. After all, it wasn't as if he and Jenna were a couple and she was off-limits to other guys. Hoping to smooth over his uncharacteristic behavior, he took the seat next to their guest. "So, what've you been up to?"

While Heath kept them entertained with stories from the Great White North, Scott was careful not to look over at Jenna too often. Heath was pretty sharp, and if he sensed there was something going on between the two of them, Scott would never hear the end of it. He still wasn't entirely certain how he felt about her, but one thing he knew for sure.

He didn't want to talk to anyone about it.

"Tell me," Heath said while he piled food on his plate. "Who drew the short straw and ended up with that old sawmill truck?"

Scott chuckled. "That'd be me."

"How's it running?"

"Off and on, like always. Why? Are you offering to help me fix it for real?"

"Sure." Grinning, Heath added, "It's not every day I get to work on something that should've been put on display at the Smithsonian before I was born. I'm off Thursday, so I could take a look at it then."

"Works for me. I'm staying out at the old homestead these days, so come by whenever it works for you."

With that settled, they joined the general conversation. Heath contributed the same easygoing wit Scott recalled from their high school days, but he couldn't miss the fact that it had a different quality now. Forced almost, as if his old friend was trying very hard to make everyone believe he was the same confident, chipper guy he'd been back then.

Before he could give that any further thought, Jenna yawned behind her hand and stood up. "I hate to be the first one to leave, but I've got an early start in the morning. Thanks so much for everything, guys. I had a great time."

"I'll walk you back to your van," Scott offered, standing to join her. Once she circled the group with goodbye hugs, he fell into step beside her as they headed for Arabesque. "Driving the dog portrait to Roanoke tomorrow, right?"

"Yeah. It's a hike, and I figure the sooner I go, the sooner I'll be back."

"Makes sense."

"Your friend Heath seems nice," she ventured with a sidelong glance. "I can just imagine all the trouble you two caused in high school."

"Yeah, we were quite the pair," he agreed with a chuckle. "I'm glad Paul invited him over. I can't remember the last time I had so much fun."

"So, you're not a natural hermit. It's good to know you can actually kick back and enjoy yourself once in a while." Playfully punching his arm, she flashed him a smile.

"It all depends on who I'm with," he replied as they stopped near her van. The early moonlight was reflected in her eyes, and he gave in to a smile of his own. "I always have fun when I'm with you."

"I'm sure you say that to all the girls."

"Not hardly." He knew his fascination with her must be easy to see, but he no longer cared. Moving slowly, he leaned in to brush a kiss over her lips. They curved in a way he felt rather than saw, and he drew back to rest his forehead on hers. "I really wish you could stay for the summer."

"Well, I'm here now. Let's make the most of it."

Dialing up the wattage on her smile, she reached up to his cheek and drew him back in for another, deeper kiss. He wrapped his arms around her and held her close, savoring that one perfect moment with her. Wishing it could last, but understanding why that kind of relationship wasn't possible for them.

For tonight at least, he and Jenna were together, and everything was right with his world. He'd worry about the rest tomorrow.

Chapter Nine

When a delivery truck pulled up in front of Jenna's studio Thursday afternoon, Gretchen looked up from her drawing with curiosity. "Were you expecting something?"

"My friend Kurt must've finished our stained-glass sheets," Jenna answered, wiping her hands on a paint rag. "He said they were a real challenge, so I can't wait to see how they turned out."

The deliveryman carefully rolled the heavily padded panes inside and glanced around. "Wow, this is quite the place. Must be fun working in here every day."

It was, Jenna agreed silently. Ever since the other night, when Scott surprised her with a kiss and a thinly veiled request to stay longer, she hadn't been able to think about much else. Renewing her lease would be simple enough, and if she put out the word that she'd be around, she would have more work than she could manage.

Unfortunately, that nagging voice in the back of her mind kept piping up to remind her of all the reasons she should move on. That list was long, but on the other side of the ledger was one very important reason to ignore them all. Scott.

Pushing aside those conflicting thoughts, she signed the driver's clipboard and handed him a tip. "Thanks for being so careful with them."

"Well, they're labeled Fragile," he pointed out, tipping his cap and pivoting his hand truck on its wheels on his way to the door. "You ladies have a good day."

Gretchen was bouncing from one sneaker

to the other like a kid waiting to meet her new puppy. Looking from the tantalizing packages to Jenna, she asked, "Can we open them now?"

Trusting that Kurt had protected his hand-iwork to the nth degree, Jenna nodded. They peeled away layer after layer of Bub-ble Wrap until the large worktable held four large sheets of glass nestled in thick card-board frames to keep the edges safe. Em-erald, cobalt, crimson and gold, the colors had so much depth, they almost seemed to breathe.

"They're gorgeous." Staring at them as if they were precious jewels, Gretchen reached her hands out to touch the most beautiful raw material Jenna had ever gotten to work with. "It's almost a shame to cut them, isn't it?"

Her sensitivity was touching, and Jenna patted her shoulder in approval. "Not many people would see it that way."

"You mean kids," the girl corrected her

with a crooked grin. "I know folks think teenagers are nothing but trouble, but that's not true."

Laughing, Jenna tugged her assistant's French braid. "Yeah, you're pretty okay. Let's take some pictures before we slice this stuff up."

They each posed for the other to get a few shots, then laid out the templates they'd designed based on the Welsh chapel Gretchen had uncovered during her research on the Barretts. They'd basically be breaking the glass, so while they traced, they adjusted the markings to ensure the brittle material would crack along lines as straight as possible.

It was painstaking work, but before long they had the makings of the tree that stood in the corner of the original window. Then Jenna took a deep breath and sent up a quick prayer for a steady hand as she began running a razor-sharp knife along the markings. When the outline of a piece was complete, she snapped it free and handed it to Gretchen, who dry fitted it in place.

Using the lead dividers that would hold the design together, they worked on opposite sides, slipping in the different colors like puzzle pieces. Consulting the map, they agreed they'd gotten everything in its proper place. After a quick snack, Jenna picked up the soldering gun that had been heating and prepared to lock in the first area. Reconsidering, she stopped midair and offered the gun to Gretchen.

"Are you serious?" she squeaked. "What if I mess it up?"

"Then we pluck it out, clean it off and start over. You're the one who did the legwork that made this possible. You should have the honors."

"Okay."

Rubbing her hands on her jeans, Gretchen took the gun and bent over the incomplete frame. She was so intent on her task, she didn't seem to notice Jenna recording her until she stood up to stretch out her back. "Are you making a video of me?"

"Yes, I am. But if it makes you nervous, I'll stop."

"No, it's fine." Clearly flattered, she added a cute giggle. "Could I get a copy and put it online? My friends would think it was cool."

Jenna couldn't see a problem with that, so she nodded. "Just don't get distracted. Kurt's getting ready to join the Renaissance fair circuit and he doesn't have time for any more glassmaking till fall."

"I thought you were leaving soon, too," Gretchen commented, glancing around the studio that still appeared to be more or less the way it was last week. "It doesn't look to me like you're going anywhere."

While Jenna wasn't normally the confiding type, she wasn't one to hide things from people, either. Over the past couple of weeks, Gretchen had proven to be responsible and trustworthy. She was keeping her grades up while spending her after-school hours helping Jenna with everything from prepping canvas frames to painting subtle details into local landscapes.

"Can you keep a secret?" she asked. When the girl nodded eagerly, she went on. "I'm thinking about staying here awhile longer."

"That would be so awesome! I thought you were set on doing the art festivals, though. What made you change your mind?"

So many things, Jenna thought, but one rose head and shoulders above the others. Literally. When she smiled, her assistant giggled again. "Oh, I get it. It's Scott."

"Not entirely," Jenna protested, then gave it up and laughed herself. "Okay, mostly. But I liked the town and the folks here even before I met him. You should never do anything just for a guy," she cautioned sternly. "Suit yourself first, and you'll have more to offer other people."

"Yeah, that's what Mrs. Barrett says, too. Both of them, actually."

"Diane and Olivia are two of the smartest

women I've ever met," Jenna said warmly. "No matter how old you get, you won't ever go wrong following their advice."

Gretchen's enthusiasm faded, and a wistful expression took its place. "Sometimes I really miss my mom."

Jenna's heart lurched unexpectedly, and she took a moment to let the lingering bitterness wash over her and move on. It had been years, but every now and then those old hurts sneaked up on her and knocked her off balance. When she felt more solid, she said, "I know, honey. This probably doesn't help you much, but I think she's missing out on a great kid."

"Thanks." Adding a watery smile, Gretchen seemed to gather herself and then focused back on their project. "Do you think we have time to do another section?"

Picking up on her desire to change the subject, Jenna decided it was best to follow her lead. "Sure. Which one do you want to do next?"

Gretchen chose to finish the meadow comprised mostly of green with a few slender shards of other colors dotted in as flowers. While they worked, they talked about her friends and school, especially a couple of boys who'd started paying more attention to the new girl. The easygoing conversation reminded Jenna of her old friend Vicky, whose parents had been generous enough to take in an abandoned sixteen-year-old and make sure she finished high school.

It had been a while since she last called them, Jenna realized, although they frequently traded jokes and news online. With Mother's Day coming up, she made a mental note to get a card for the kindhearted teacher who'd been more like a mother to her than the woman who'd passed along her talent but not much of anything else. Sometimes, Jenna thought that was a good thing.

Other times, like Gretchen, she missed her mom. They'd shared some good stretches when they hadn't been bugging out in the middle of the night to avoid paying back rent to an angry landlord. Jenna dimly recalled trips to the beach at sunset to paint, and a day at a county fair when she'd ridden a gentle draft horse named Gideon, who had been the biggest creature she'd ever seen. There were other positive memories, too, but sadly they were few and far between.

All of them put together couldn't balance out the fact that one night her mother had simply walked out of her life. Discouraged by her own inability to forgive and forget, Jenna sent up a fervent prayer that someday Gretchen would find a way to come to terms with her past and be happy.

"So," Heath began while he checked another spark plug and tossed it on the growing pile of junk parts on the ground. "Jenna Reed seems nice."

Hard as he'd been trying, Scott was having a tough time masking his feelings for the bright, bubbly artist. Finally, he gave up and relented with a grin. "She is."

"And you like her." Yanking a worn-out hose from its spot, his old buddy scowled at it and added it to the others. The new one didn't want to go on, but he persuaded it into place with a grunt of satisfaction. Resting his forearms on the fender, he said, "Paul said you and Jenna are just friends, but it didn't look that way to me the other night. What's really going on with you two?"

As it had so many times, Scott's mind wandered back to that evening, and he couldn't help smiling. While he wasn't impulsive by nature, kissing Jenna had been a leap that had taken him by surprise. That she'd returned it was even more astonishing, and he hadn't quite figured out what that meant.

It might have been a sweet gesture from someone he'd been spending most of his free time with. Then again, when he considered the fact that he kept wishing she'd rethink her summer plans, he couldn't help wondering if there was something developing between them, after all.

One thing he couldn't deny: holding her that way had felt right to him. No matter how many times he rolled that scene around in his head, he couldn't find a single thing wrong with it. The problem was it made him wish for more nights like that one, laughing and talking with her, listening when she had something to tell him.

Ending with a kiss that promised more if he wanted them. Which he did, in spite of his persistent doubts about diving into a serious relationship anytime soon. Like the homestead, his life was in a precarious state right now, teetering in that gray zone between feeling solid and caving in on him.

Was it right to ask someone else to take that on when he wasn't even sure he wanted it himself? He carefully followed the terms of his parole, never getting close to crossing a line that might extend his sentence even one more day. The officer in charge of his case filed glowing reports of Scott's efforts and had assured him that if he continued the way he had been, this time next year he'd be a totally free man.

And then what? Scott mused while he cracked open a set of new spark plugs and handed one of them to Heath. Paul asking him to start a new line of furniture for the family business was as gratifying for Scott as it was out of the blue. His modest inheritance wouldn't last forever, so eventually he'd need a job. Finding work was the toughest challenge for ex-cons, and if he signed on at the mill, he wouldn't have to worry about scraping by as a temporary laborer somewhere.

"Dime for your thoughts," Heath suggested without looking at him.

"Isn't it a penny?"

"Smart as you are?" the mechanic chuckled. "A dime seems more like it. You don't have to tell me," he added, glancing over before focusing back on the plugs. "But if you're looking for an ear, I'm a pretty good listener."

Why not? Scott decided, going on to fill his old friend in. Heath was mostly quiet, nodding and "hmming" just often enough to keep the one-way conversation moving. When he'd touched on all the details, Scott ended with something he rarely did: he asked Heath for his opinion. "What would *you* do?"

"Take the job and put a ring on Jenna's finger before someone else does."

"Is that advice or a threat?" When his friend grinned, Scott laughed. "I knew you liked her just a little too much."

"What's not to like? She's pretty and talented and she's got a great sense of humor. Women like that don't just fall outta the sky, y'know." Setting down his tools, he wiped his hands on a rag and asked, "How'd you two get together, anyway?"

Scott relayed their unusual meeting,

and Heath gave him an odd sidelong look. "You're serious, aren't you?"

"Yeah. Why?"

"You don't think that's some kind of a hint? Like, from Will?"

"That's nuts," he protested with a short laugh. "I think you've been under the hood with that engine so long the gas vapors are getting to you."

Heath shrugged. "Suit yourself, but I'm telling you stranger things have happened."

"Not to me."

"Well, now," he muttered as he dipped back under the hood. "That's a shame."

Scott had no clue what the guy was talking about, and he didn't want to. But while they continued working, he couldn't shake the eerie feeling that   as much as he hated to believe it—Heath just might have a point.

His grandfather had left him not only a place to live, but seed money and something to occupy his time until he got fully back on his feet. Generous and pragmatic, the solution had enabled him to regain his bearings and his pride. Both had taken a real beating these past few years, and he'd always be grateful to the man who'd figured out what Scott needed most and made sure it was waiting for him when he returned to Barrett's Mill.

Unsettling at it was to acknowledge such an unusual possibility, one thing was certain. If God had assigned him a guardian angel to help him rebuild his life, Scott couldn't have asked for anyone better than Granddad.

"Okay," he allowed with a sigh. "Maybe you're right."

"Of course I am. You could've met up with one of the little old ladies from church planting those flowers at the cemetery. They're sweet, but not exactly your type," he added with a goofy grin.

They both laughed, and Scott was struck by how good it felt to be joking around with his childhood friend again. They'd last seen each other a few weeks after graduation, promising to stay in touch after they went their separate ways. They hadn't.

Frowning, he said, "I'm sorry I didn't keep in touch. I wish—"

"Don't sweat it." Heath waved off his apology with another grin. "Life happens to all of us."

It turned out Jenna had it right, he thought: when he gave them a chance, most people were more than ready to forgive him. "Yeah, it does. Thanks for understanding, though."

"No problem. Now, let's get this thing put back together and see if all this knuckle bashing was worth it."

When they had finished reassembling the ancient engine, Scott noticed something glinting in the grass. He leaned down and picked up a stray nut and bolt, neatly threaded together. When he held them up, Heath glared at him and he glared back. "What? I didn't drop 'em on purpose."

His buddy held out a grease-stained hand

and after Scott gave the pieces to him, he scanned their work before dropping them into his pocket. "They're extra."

"Are you sure?"

"No, but I figure this thing can't run any worse now than it did before."

"Good point," Scott agreed with a chuckle. "Let's give it a shot."

Climbing in, he crossed his fingers and turned the key. With a little coaxing, the engine started and Heath adjusted the fuel and air combination so the truck settled into a throaty but steady rumble. Just to be safe, they tried it a couple more times with the same encouraging results.

Heath leaned his arms on the open driver's window. "Sounds better, but it could use some more TLC. I can come by again next Thursday, if you want."

"I hate to hog all your free time," Scott protested.

"Don't worry about it. It's not like I've got anything else going on these days."

Something flitted through his eyes, and Scott recognized it instantly: regret. He'd seen it frequently in his mirror, though not so much lately. Opening up to Jenna had seemed to chase away most of those shadows, and he thought maybe he could do the same for Heath. "Anything you wanna tell me?"

Grimacing, Heath shook his head. "I appreciate you asking, though."

Scott knew better than to push him for more and got out of the truck to help Heath gather up his tools. "If you change your mind, let me know."

"Okay." The somber look gave way to his usual aw-shucks grin. "I'm glad you came back, Scott. It's nice to hang out with someone who knows not to hassle me about stuff."

He'd voiced exactly what Scott was thinking, and he grinned back as they walked toward Heath's shiny pickup. "Same here. Not to mention I'll be driving this truck for a while, so it'll be handy to have a mechanic who doesn't mind getting paid with Gram's triple-berry pie."

"It's like a wonder food," he agreed as he climbed up into the cab and looked out the window at Scott. "It goes with everything."

"Sure does. Have a good one."

Lifting his hand in reply, Heath drove down the dirt lane and pulled onto the road that led back to town. Now that he was alone, Scott realized he'd been up since the crack of dawn and was feeling every hour of sleep he'd lost fretting over what to do about Jenna. With sunlight warming his yard and a nice breeze blowing through the boughs overhead, he stretched out at the foot of an ancient oak and promptly fell asleep.

The sound of tires crunching on gravel roused him just enough to crack open one eye so he could see who was coming up the driveway. When he saw Jenna's van, he smothered a grin and pretended to keep on snoozing. Her sneakers made barely a sound in the grass, but the telltale scent of her—paint thinner and something flowery—floated in on the breeze.

It was uniquely her, and he knew that for the rest of his life when he smelled either of those two things, he'd think of the kindhearted artist who'd rescued him from himself.

She paused beside him, and he could almost picture her folding her arms as she stared down at him, trying to decide if she should wake him or not. Suddenly, cold water and ice cubes rained down on him, and he bolted upright, sputtering and caught completely off guard.

"What're you doing?" He'd meant for it to come out as a growl, but there was more laughter in it than anything.

"You're not fooling anyone lying there like Boyd on a lazy day," she informed him with a knowing smirk. "I saw you watching me."

Busted, he thought as he sluiced water from his hair with his hands and dried them on his jeans. "Think you're pretty smart, don't you?"

"Most of the time."

Quite honestly, he had a sneaking suspicion she was smarter than he was. Not long ago, admitting that would have galled him, but for some reason with her, it turned out to be a pleasant surprise. One of the many she'd sprung on him, actually. "So, what're you doing all the way out here?"

"I was doing some touch-ups on the signage at the mill, so I thought I'd stop and see how things are coming along here." Those summer-sky eyes drifted from the chapel to the house and then settled on him with a curious gleam. "Do you have time to show me around?"

"Sure." He always had time for a woman who brightened his days the way she did, but he decided to keep that very personal revelation to himself. They'd taken a few tentative steps toward each other, but he still wasn't at all certain where things with Jenna might lead. For now, he was content to go along with the suggestion she'd made the other night and spend as much time with her as he could.

"I finished up the chapel roof yesterday," he explained, pointing to the new shingles that made the weathered old clapboards look even shabbier than they had before. "Next is paint and new shutters, both white."

"And you finished the steps," she noted as they went up them into the small sanctuary.

"Poured new footers and rebuilt 'em from scratch," he commented with more than a little pride. "They oughta last another hundred years or so."

"Will would be so proud of you," she approved, doing a slow circuit of the nearly completed interior. "I'm glad you went with hand-hewn boards on the walls. In a few years, they'll age and look like the old ones did."

He'd ripped them himself over at the mill and carted them back in the old truck that had probably made the same trip countless times back in the day. Telling her that would sound like bragging, though, and that really wasn't his style anymore. So he just smiled and thanked her.

Not much got by her, and she tilted her head with a knowing look. "You milled them yourself, didn't you?"

"Well...yeah. The crew's real busy, so I went in after hours and cherry-picked the leftovers for this place. I gotta be honest, getting the waterwheel fired up to run the saws was the hardest part," he confided with a chuckle. "Paul showed me how to do it, and it's not that complicated. The old works didn't give him a lick of trouble, but I'm telling you that thing hates me."

"Tourists love it, though. When all the saws are going, the whole building shakes, and you can't hear anything else above all that racket. It's really cool, especially when you realize it was all built by hand and gets its power from little old Sterling Creek."

She pointed out one of the window openings toward the stream, appreciation shining in her expressive eyes. Since coming home, Scott had reconnected with the homestead and historic sawmill the original Barretts had built so long ago. Discovering that Jenna shared his reverence for what his ancestors had accomplished only added to his growing admiration of her.

In self-defense, he pushed that dangerous thought aside and strolled over to the boarded-up opening at the front of the little church. "I still have to refinish the floor and replace the panes in the side-window grids so they open like they used to. The last piece will be your stained glass. When you and Gretchen are done putting Humpty Dumpty back together, I'll reinstall it and we'll be all set."

"It's slow, delicate work, but we're making good progress. At the rate we're going, it should be done in about a week."

And then, so would they, he added morosely. Jenna would be leaving, and Scott would be staying. More than ever, it was killing him to realize that he was basically a prisoner in his hometown until someone with legal authority told him otherwise.

Then again, even if he was allowed to leave, what would he do? Traipse around the country, following Jenna like some pathetic old hound desperate for her attention? Maybe a few years ago he could've made something like that work, but not now. That reckless part of him didn't exist anymore, and he considered that a good thing. Coming home had reminded him that he was smarter than that, and it was okay for him to let go of people and memories that caused him pain.

But letting go of Jenna…that was different. From the first time he'd met her, she'd brought nothing but good into his life. As his friend, she'd encouraged him to reconnect with his family, and then with God in a way he didn't think he could have managed on his own.

Because of his background, having the freedom to choose for himself was very important to him. Jenna deserved nothing less than that. Much as he'd love for her to stay, he'd never stand in the way of the career that meant so much to her and ask her to change her plans for him. But he wasn't keen on her leaving, either.

"You know," she began in a thoughtful tone. "Once the chapel is finished, if you trim back those trees and install some skylights, it would be an amazing workspace."

"Nah. It's kinda snug in here for my taste." When she made a face at him, he chuckled. "But speaking of finishing things, I still owe you dinner at the Spring House. Does tomorrow night work for you?"

"Sure." Glancing down at her ratty jeans and paint-spattered sneakers, she laughed. "I'm guessing this won't do, though. Amy's way smaller than me, but maybe I can borrow something girlie from Chelsea."

"She'd be the one to ask. When I have a reservation, I'll call and let you know what time."

"Sounds good." They stood there just staring at each other for several awkward seconds. Rocking back on her heels, she cast another look around before coming back to him. "Was there anything else you wanted to show me?"

"Not really, but I've got a fresh batch of sweet tea. Would you like some?"

"Oh, that Southern hospitality," she teased while they strolled toward the house. "I'm really gonna miss it."

"You don't have to. You could hang around and keep enjoying it."

Where had that come from? he wondered with a silent groan. Sure, he'd been thinking along those lines for days now, but he'd been careful not to say anything that would give her the impression he objected to her leaving. Even though he did. Leery of making the situation worse, he figured the best approach was to pretend he hadn't said anything.

For her part, Jenna didn't comment on his careless slipup. But she did give him a long, pensive look before heading toward the back door.

"You don't have to go that way anymore." He rested a foot on the bottom step of the front porch and stomped on the solid riser. "All fixed."

This look was curious, and she went ahead of him onto the porch. It was still rough, but he'd taken advantage of his new position at the mill and had snagged a couple of Adirondack-style chairs and a small table with his employee discount. "I haven't decided whether to paint or stain them, or just leave them be and seal them. What do you think?"

Sitting in the farther one, she ran a hand over the smooth pine surface and smiled.

"I think they're perfect just like this. You know, if you painted this place yellow, it would be a nice bright spot here in the middle of all these trees. It would also look a lot like my dream house."

He'd been leaning that way, anyway, so her comment settled it for him. Not that he was thinking about her spending more time here, of course. It was just that he didn't have much experience with—or interest in—decorating, and he valued her artistic opinion. "Yellow's a good color, so that works for me."

"And this yard is a disaster. It needs... something."

"It needs a lot of somethings," he agreed with a chuckle. "But landscaping's not exactly my strong point."

"It's not that hard." Illustrating with a sweep of her hand, she went on. "You've already worn a path up to the house from the driveway, so it would be easy to dig that out and lay some gravel. Then you plant flowers on either side, leading up to the porch to welcome your guests."

"You're the only one who's ever sat up here besides me," he pointed out.

"Maybe more folks would visit if this place felt more inviting," she shot back in the direct approach he'd come to value so much from her. "Once you hack all the weeds out of the old gardens, you could transplant some of the wildflowers from over the hill in here. Then add a few hanging baskets and voilà! Pretty cottage in the woods."

"You mean like in all those old fairy tales?"

"Minus the mean old witch, of course."

"Of course," he echoed with a grin. An idea for spending a little extra time with her popped into his head, and he added, "Tell you what. Since I'm clueless about flowers and stuff, I'll pay for the supplies you need, and you can do whatever you want here."

"Seriously?"

"Yup. Not only will it look nice, but it'll get Mom off my back about sprucing up the gardens."

"Cool. I'm in."

"I'll go get us some drinks, and we'll toast to it. Be right back."

Going through the house only reinforced his impression of what a mess it still was. He'd tinkered around in the kitchen and bathroom enough that they functioned fairly well, but they were decades from being classified as modern. Now that the chapel was more or less done, he could turn his attention to making the cottage more than barely livable.

An added bonus was that the rehab would keep his mind off how much he was going to miss Jenna when she left later this month. Then again, he wasn't sure there was enough work for him anywhere to accomplish that.

Chapter Ten

That evening, a classic roadster she'd never seen pulled into the turnaround in front of Jenna's studio. People often stopped to ask for directions, so she expected that to be the case this time. When Scott stepped out, she couldn't help laughing. "Did Heath turn that old mill truck into this cute little thing?"

"He's good, but not that good. He did loan me this so we wouldn't be embarrassed to pull under the front portico with all those fancy cars at the Spring House. Glad you like it."

"It's adorable." The paint job was clearly

in progress, but it promised to be a cheerful canary yellow. "What kind is it?"

"MG, late sixties, I think he said. Fred Morgan took it in trade for some body-work he did for a customer a while back, and Heath bought it from him as a project. It's totally safe to drive," Scott added, as if she needed reassurance.

"I'm sure it is. I trust you." The relief on his face told her just how much he needed to hear that from her. Smiling, she ran a hand over the battered ragtop. "Does this go down?"

He chuckled. "Yeah, but then you can't get it back up. The motor's been back-ordered from some supplier in England for a month now, and Heath's not thrilled about it."

"It'll be really cute when it's all fixed up. Can I drive?"

"The steering wheel's on the right."

"I can see that," she shot back.

"Can you handle a manual transmission?" When she gave him a withering look, he chuckled. "Okay, then." He opened the door with a flourish and swung it closed behind her. Leaning down, he grinned at her through the open window. "You look incredible, by the way."

Male admiration glimmered in his dark eyes, and Jenna felt a blush creeping over her cheeks. Chelsea had insisted the pale blue dress looked stunning on her, but it was flattering to hear that Scott's assessment of her outfit matched her friend's. "Thanks. I don't get dressed up very often."

"How come?"

"I don't have much reason to, I guess. Trousers and a blouse are fine for church, and other than that, I'm usually making a mess with something or other in my studio."

"So you're saying you need to get out more?"

What was the right answer to that? she wondered. If she said yes, he might think she was hinting for another date with him. If she said no, he might assume she didn't want another one. To be on the safe side, she smiled. "Don't we all?"

That made him laugh, and while he circled the car to get in, she congratulated herself on evading some potentially dangerous social quicksand. Her anxiety made no sense whatsoever, she chided herself while she adjusted the rearview and familiarized herself with the old-style manual controls. She and Scott saw each other almost every day, and she knew him better than she'd known most of her former boyfriends.

"Jenna?" When she looked over, he grimaced. "Are you as nervous as I am?"

"Yes," she breathed, relieved to discover she wasn't the only one. "Stupid, right?"

"I didn't mean to make things weird between us by asking you out."

His apologetic tone wiped away the last of her misgivings, and she gave him her brightest smile. "It's not weird, just different. Good different," she added quickly.

"How did you know I was gonna ask you that?"

"Reading people is one of my hobbies, remember?" She started the car and drove around the semicircle out to the road. "For the record, you don't make it easy."

Staring out his window, he let out a heavy sigh. "Yeah, I get that a lot."

"Fortunately for you, I love a good challenge."

He gave her a sidelong glance, but didn't say anything. When she replayed her last comment in her mind, she realized he might have misinterpreted what she'd meant by it. The trouble was anything she came up with to explain it away sounded lame, so she decided it was best to let it go.

Weaving gently on the gravel road, she said, "This little baby handles like a dream. Once it's a convertible again, Heath shouldn't have any problem selling it."

"I'll tell him you said so."

The restaurant was in nearby Cambridge,

and during the short drive they chatted back and forth about their various projects. They arrived long before they ran out of things to talk about, and Jenna was almost disappointed that it was time to hand the sunny little car over to a valet.

She'd lived in cities and towns all over the country, and she'd seen her share of upscale restaurants. With its gracious antebellum architecture and expansive grounds, the Spring House had a charm all its own. In the distance she heard a splash and followed the sound to find a couple of geese touching down on a pond that also was home to two graceful white swans.

When she noticed something swimming in the water behind them, she barely contained a squeal. "They had babies!"

Tiny gray versions of their parents, four cygnets trailed after them in a straggly formation that made them seem all the more precious. When Scott suggested they go take a look, she agreed instantly. Careful to avoid making too much noise, they crept toward the bank and stood quietly while the swan family made their circuit of the modest-size pond.

"Aren't they beautiful?" she sighed.

"Very."

Something in his tone caught her attention, and she looked up to find him smiling at her. "What?"

"I just think it's cool how you get so excited about stuff like this. With all you've been through, I'd expect you to be more jaded."

"Beauty is in the details, the small things most people don't really pick up on. My old art teacher used to say that, and it's one of the best lessons she taught me."

"And now you've taught it to me." Reaching out, he grasped both of her hands loosely in his and smiled. "That means more to me than I could ever say."

The tender current running beneath his words conveyed a deeper sentiment, and she blinked at him while her mind spun in circles hunting for a response. As usual, her heart took over, and she leaned in to brush a kiss over his lips. It was a bold move, one she didn't normally make, but judging by the emotion glittering in his eyes it had been the right one.

"I'm really gonna miss you," he said gruffly, leaning his forehead against hers with a dejected sigh. She'd handled this kind of situation many times, and usually she offered pragmatism with a dash of sympathy.

This time, though, she let her heart take the lead. "You know, since that barbecue at Paul and Chelsea's, I've been thinking."

He pulled his head back, and she saw a spark of hope brighten his gloomy features. "About?"

"Staying here for a while longer. I could renew the lease on my studio and generate some business with the tourists who come into town to see the sawmill. I turned away a bunch of local contracts because I couldn't be sure I'd be here to do them. I'd imagine those people would still be interested in working with me."

The optimism that had warmed his eyes cooled a bit. "I'm not sure what my plans are, Jenna. Don't stay because of me."

"Arrogant, aren't you?" she teased, laughing to let him know she was joking. "I've never done anything for a guy, and I've got no intention of starting now. That was my mom's approach to life, and if I learned anything from her, it's that those kind of compromises never end up the way you want them to."

She hadn't meant to voice that last part out loud, but her earlier conversation with Gretchen had left thoughts of her own absent mother lodged in an uncomfortable position at the front of her mind. The compassion in Scott's eyes made her wish she'd kept her personal issues to herself. "You miss her sometimes, don't you?"

"A little, maybe." Fiddling with his tie,

she glanced up at him, hoping to make him understand. "I wish things had turned out differently is all. Since they didn't, I try not to think too much about what might have been."

"I can relate to that."

Spoken without the bitterness that had been so much a part of him when they'd first met, those words told her just how far he'd come during these past few weeks. She was so proud of him, but she didn't know how to phrase it properly. Instead, she dangled her arms over those strong shoulders and gave him a lazy smile. "So, how would you feel if I stuck around a little longer?"

"It's a good idea, business-wise, since you've already got clients in the area. Cambridge hosts art shows over the summer, and so do lots of the other towns around here."

"Don't bore me with all that practical stuff," she chided gently. "I asked how you'd *feel*."

He hesitated, clearly torn between remaining detached from her and being honest. After a long silence he bent to kiss her, adding one of those mellow smiles she'd come to adore. "I'd love it if you stayed."

"That's settled, then," she agreed with a laugh. "To celebrate, I think we should have the lobster."

"Whatever you want. But first, I want to thank you."

"For what? Emptying your wallet?"

"For being the last thing I expected," he corrected her in a gentle voice. Sweeping her hair back over her shoulder, he went on. "When I finally came home, I was set on keeping to myself and waiting for the dust around me to settle. You wouldn't let me do that, and I'll always be grateful to you for not letting me get by with the hermit thing."

"Oh, eventually some girl would've come along and dragged you out of your cave. You're way too good-looking to be a hermit."

Frowning now, he shook his head. "I'm

serious, Jenna. Outside of my family, no one's ever put in as much effort with me as you have. I wish I knew how to thank you."

"You just did."

Flashing him her very best smile, she impulsively hugged him. After a moment, his arms came around her, pulling her close enough that she could feel his heart beat against her cheek. That very first day in the cemetery, she'd glimpsed this magnificent heart, broken and weary but still willing to try.

In her mind, that was the definition of courage. Falling but struggling back to your feet to keep on climbing because you simply refused to give up. Standing there, wrapped in Scott's arms, it dawned on her that he was the bravest man she'd ever met. It wouldn't take much for her to fall hard for him, and if he'd been any other guy she'd known, this would be the point where she would bolt and never look back.

But not now, because for the first time

her heart and head were in complete agreement about a man. Knowing that should have scared her half to death, but she was astonished to find she felt quite the opposite. And it was wonderful.

Sighing in contentment, she said, "It's such a beautiful evening. I wish we didn't have to go inside."

"We don't," he replied, dropping a kiss on the top of her head. "I finagled us a table on the patio."

Stunned by the surprise, she stared up at him in disbelief. "Those tables are always booked way in advance. How did you manage that?"

"The owner's a friend of my parents'." Stepping back, he took her hand and started walking toward the flagstone patio bordered by gorgeous magnolia trees draped in tiny white lights. "I don't have many connections around here these days, but the ones I do have are golden."

He slid her a mischievous grin that made her laugh.

"So I'm on your short list?"

"You could say that, I guess."

The grin had vanished, replaced by something far less appealing. His quick shift from teasing to serious reminded her that while he might come across as cockier than most, there was still a bruised spirit hiding behind all that Barrett bravado. Sensing he needed a boost, she hugged his arm as they followed the meandering path up from the pond. "That's really sweet, Scott. Thank you."

"You're welcome."

This time, his smile came across much softer, as if he'd invented it just for her. That was ridiculous, of course, but she couldn't deny that it reinforced her decision to forego the art circuit this summer. She had no idea where things with Scott and her might be going, but instinct told her she'd have a blast finding out.

Before they got to the edge of the patio, a middle-aged man in a dark suit approached them, arms open while he smiled. He looked like a generous old uncle delighted to have them for company, rather than someone with a restaurant full of paying customers to look after. "Scott, how are you?"

"Fine, Lyle," he replied as they shook hands. Nudging Jenna forward with his other arm, he added, "Lyle Carrington, this is Jenna Reed."

"A pleasure to meet you, my dear. How are you both doing this lovely evening?"

"Just fine," Scott answered smoothly. "And you?"

"Everyone in the family's happy and healthy, so I can't complain." Turning to Jenna, he took her hand in an old-fashioned gentleman's manner that brought to mind those classic black-and-white movies she still enjoyed. Fortunately for her, he stopped short of kissing it. "Welcome to the Spring House."

"Thanks so much for fitting us in. I've been wanting to eat here for months."

Crooking a finger, he motioned her closer and whispered, "Don't tell anyone, but we always keep a couple of tables stashed away for good friends. When we're full, we just pull them out of storage and set them up where we have space. That way, we never have to turn away our favorite people."

The fond smile he gave Scott was totally genuine, and if they hadn't been in the midst of a crowd, Jenna would have hugged the kind man on the spot. Since that would certainly embarrass Scott to no end, she settled for something a little safer. "It's always nice when someone makes you feel special."

"Special," Lyle scoffed, waving away the thought. Grasping Scott's shoulder, he explained, "This one's my godson. A handful, Lord knows, but well worth the effort. If you'll follow me, I'll get you seated and bring you some menus."

While they walked behind him, Jenna murmured, "Your godfather owns the Spring House?"

"Yup."

"How could you neglect to mention that when I was gushing about this place at The Whistlestop?"

A slow, mischievous grin moved across his face, and she laughed. "You called Lyle that day, didn't you?"

"Pretty much."

She couldn't decide if Scott was sneaky or clever, but since she was finally getting to experience the grand estate for herself, she decided she didn't care all that much. Lyle made a show of seating her and then informed Scott he was perfectly capable of pulling out his own chair. Beaming at a couple seated nearby, he stopped to chat with them on his way inside. And the next couple and the next, so it took him nearly five minutes to leave the patio.

"Hope you're not in a hurry to get home

tonight," Scott joked as he dismantled the elegant napkin fashioned to look like a swan. "At this rate, it could take a while to get our menus."

"I don't mind a bit. It gives me more time to admire everything."

While she took in their surroundings, she noticed a huge white tent down near the edge of the pond. Lights had been strung on poles, leading out from a side door of the main restaurant. Music filtered out through the canvas doors that had been tied back with humongous pink bows. While she watched, a bride and groom paused on the flagstone stairs that led to the tent from the top of a slight rise.

Her white gown swirled around her like a cloud, and she held a bouquet of pink roses mixed with other flowers, cascading from her hands down the front of her dress. With the groom dressed in black tails, they looked as if they'd just stepped off the top of a wedding cake. They shared a quick kiss, and as they joined their guests, laughter trailed behind them in a joyous wake that would have melted the iciest heart on earth.

"You okay?"

Scott's question dragged her attention back to their table, and she nodded. "Why?"

"You just sighed. Is that the kind of reception you want someday?" he asked, motioning toward the tent with his water goblet.

"Oh, I don't know. I never really thought about it."

She knew he was on the cynical side, but the look he was giving her now was one of the most skeptical she'd ever seen. "Aw, come on. Every girl starts thinking about her wedding day at some point. Like eight years old."

"Not me."

Setting down his glass, he leaned in to speak more quietly. "You're telling me you never dressed Barbie all in white, plopped a tissue on her head and dragged poor, unsuspecting Ken to the altar?"

"Never." Not that she hadn't wanted to, she amended silently. It was just that her mother's wretched track record with men had soured Jenna on happily-ever-after a long time ago. That seemed a little melodramatic, so she settled for something less dire. "Mom wasn't the marrying kind, and I guess I inherited that from her."

"For better or worse?"

She appreciated his attempt to lighten the difficult subject for her, and she grinned. "Right."

Leaning back in his chair, Scott studied her for several long, uncomfortable moments. Just when she was about to change tracks, a young woman floated over to hand them menus and recite a list of specials. When she was finished, she didn't have to wait long for them to order.

Glancing over at Jenna, Scott raised an eyebrow. "Lobster?"

"Absolutely."

Facing the waitress, he held up two fingers in a V, and she nodded. "Excellent choice, sir."

After confirming they were happy drinking water, she floated back the way she'd come. Jenna had watched Scott closely, gauging how much attention he paid to the attractive server. She'd learned a lot about former boyfriends that way, and she was pleased that he seemed completely indifferent to the young woman. Jenna recognized that her strategy was immature, but in the past it had proven very effective.

"I'm not checking her out," Scott assured her with one of those aggravating grins of his. "Even if I wasn't here with you, I wouldn't be interested. She's not my type."

She recognized that he was baiting her, but she couldn't see any harm in biting. "Really? And what is your type?"

In answer, he took the salt and pepper off their silver tray and spun it so the polished back of it reflected her face back at her. It was a clever way to answer her question, and she fanned her face in Southern belle fashion. Hauling out her best honeyed accent, she drawled, "How you do flatter me, sir. I may faint."

"Not to worry, darlin'," he drawled back, a wicked glint lighting his eyes. "If you fall, I'll catch you."

They both broke up laughing and clinked their water goblets over the hurricane lamp in the center of the table. "You know, I keep meaning to ask you something. When I was in L.A. last year, I met a Tess Barrett at one of the art festivals. She reminds me a lot of you and your brothers. Any chance you're related somehow?"

"My cousin," he replied with a nod. "We've never met, though."

"Why not?"

"I'm not sure. All Dad ever said about it was Uncle George moved away years ago and never came back."

Jenna was well acquainted with family problems, so she deftly steered the conversation back to lighter topics. From that point on, the evening was a fun mixture of teasing and shoptalk, punctuated by the best lobster she'd ever eaten outside of Maine.

Despite all that, she couldn't shake the uneasy feeling that something had shifted between them. Mulling it over while they split a piccc of dccadcnt twclvc-laycr Swiss chocolate cake, she realized it had started when he'd promised to catch her if she fell.

He'd been kidding, of course, but the look he'd given her when he'd said it had told her that on some level, he meant it. For all his sarcasm, she'd learned Scott was a very serious guy who stood by what he said. This man had made a promise to watch out for her, and she didn't doubt for a second that he'd keep it.

Not long ago, the mere whisper of that kind of commitment would have made her run, determined to avoid the foolish mistakes her mother had made over and over. But tonight, for the first time in her life, Jenna was more than content to stay right where she was.

Scott stepped back from the section of weathered clapboards he'd just finished painting, trying to decide if he liked the result or not. It was a big, labor-intensive job, which was why he'd been putting it off for so long. But Jenna's comment the other day about the cottage in the woods resembling her dream house had nudged him into gear, and he'd been comparing swatches of various hues of yellow. The problem was tiny samples weren't enough to give him a true picture of how the place would look when the whole thing was that color.

So here he was, slathering on various shades with names like Daffodil and Antique Saffron. Right now, the leading contender was Southern Sunrise, but he was reserving judgment until he saw how it appeared later in the day. Normally, he was the kind of guy who figured yellow was yellow, and he was pondering why the paint mattered so much to him when a dark green pickup turned into his driveway.

Recognizing Jason, Scott capped the paint can and strolled over to meet him. "'Morning. Shouldn't you be over at the mill slaving over that redwood patio set?"

"On my way," his younger brother assured him through the open driver's window. "Just thought I'd stop and see how things are going out here."

Jason wasn't the type to come by without a reason, and Scott narrowed his eyes. "They're going. What do you want?"

"To take advantage of your expertise and good nature."

He looked totally serious, but Scott knew him well enough to get the joke about his temperament. Laughing, he said, "Right. Must mean your wife sent you out here."

"The other day, Amy saw the buffet you made for Chelsea. She went on and on about how gorgeous it is, and she's hoping you have time to make an oak headboard for our new bedroom."

"Stores sell those things, y'know."

"We've looked everywhere." The last word came out on a groan. Fishing a folded piece of paper from the pocket of his denim shirt, he handed it to Scott. "This is what she's got in mind. I'll pay for the timber, but if you can put it together, I'll owe you one."

While he considered the detailed sketch, Scott decided the intricate design was far from his own style, but he could manage it well enough. Sliding it into the back pocket of his jeans, he said, "I should be able to handle that. When does she want it?"

"You know women. ASAP."

Laughing, Scott shook his head. "You got it. And you won't owe me anything, little brother. It'll be my wedding present to you and Amy."

"Awesome! Thanks." Glancing over at the house, he commented, "I never thought this old place could look so good. It's like it's been out here all this time just waiting for someone to give it some love."

Funny, that was exactly what Scott had been thinking earlier that morning. He'd never admit that to anyone else, though, so he shrugged. "Glad you like it."

Jason's hazel eyes came back to him with an eagerness no one could possibly miss. "Does this mean you took Paul up on his offer to work at the mill?"

"For now, anyway. At least until Chelsea gets the Artisan Line up and running with someone else."

Some of Jason's enthusiasm faded, but he nodded in understanding. "Keeping your options open."

"Right."

"Well, however long you stay, it'll be nice to have a younger guy at the mill to balance out the older ones. I like 'em and everything, but they still treat me like I'm ten."

"That's what happens when you work with

people who remember you in diapers," Scott told him with a grin.

"Tell me about it. Thanks again for taking on Amy's project."

"No problem. See ya."

Holding up a hand in response, Jason backed into the turnaround and pulled onto the road that led to the mill. Watching him go, Scott was struck by just how close he now lived to where he worked. If he wanted to, he could take a quick hike through the woods and be at his job in a few minutes. Or…

Angling his head, he looked over at the newly refurbished chapel. He sensed a brainstorm coming on, and he trotted up the steps, driven by the kind of excitement he hadn't felt in a very long time.

Standing in the middle of the empty space, his head filled with the mellow scent of white oak, it wasn't hard to envision himself working in here. The blank areas between the tall windows could hold workbenches, and he pictured racks for wood storage running along the back wall on either side of the door.

As his eyes drifted upward to the patched roof, he heard Jenna's voice in his memory.

If you trimmed back those trees and installed some skylights, this would be an amazing workspace.

Suddenly, he agreed with her wholeheartedly despite the sweat he'd have to invest into making it happen. Because really, he had all the time in the world. The question was, did he want to spend so much of it creating a workshop?

If he did, he could supplement his income at the mill with a sideline of his own. Of course, that would mean putting down roots in the hometown he'd been so desperate to escape nearly ten years ago. Having seen more than his share of the world, he wasn't too proud to admit Barrett's Mill was looking pretty good to him these days. While he rolled the idea around in his mind, it started growing on him, but he firmly put on the brakes out of respect for Granddad.

How would he have felt about Scott cutting holes in the chapel roof and taking over what had been a sacred space to create a new business? The tug of new opportunity fought with his sense of duty to the generous man who'd basically left him a fresh start, and Scott was torn. He thought about visiting the cemetery in an effort to sort things out but changed his mind.

Will Barrett might be buried under the stone that bore his name, but his spirit— everything that made him who he'd been— was here. Lingering around his boyhood home, watching over Scott to make sure things were going well for him.

That sensation of having a guardian angel came over Scott again, and he sprawled out on the floor. He surveyed the blank canvas around him with a brand-new perspective, then stared up at the ceiling. "All right,

Granddad, I'm listening. What do you think I should do?"

Scott felt a little foolish, lying there waiting for some kind of answer, but he trusted his resourceful grandfather to find a way to respond.

"Sorry. Am I interrupting something?"

The sound of Jenna's voice was all the sign he needed, and he sent a grin heavenward.

"Got it," he murmured, winking at he stood to greet his unexpected—but very welcome—visitor. "Not a bit. What's up?"

"Your stained-glass window's almost done, and I want to make sure the measurements will match up. I'd hate to find out the frame is off by a quarter inch or something like that."

"If it is, I'll just cut a bigger hole." He really didn't understand the problem, but then picked up on the subtle twinkle in her blue eyes. Moving closer, he slipped his arms lightly around her. "Unless there's another reason you came by."

Flashing him a siren's smile, she tilted her cute little nose in the air. "I have no idea what you're talking about."

"Uh-huh."

A pretty blush crept over her face, and she started fiddling with the buttons on his shirt. "So what were you thinking about in here? It looked pretty serious."

You, he nearly blurted, but caught himself just in time. This woman really messed with his head, not to mention his suddenly talkative heart. But he wasn't quite ready to go there with her, so he kept his reply more businesslike. "Just wondering if Granddad would mind if I made this place into a workshop."

"You mean like I suggested a couple weeks ago?" Her eyes narrowed. "Right before you shot me down?"

Grinning, he dropped in for a quick kiss to soothe her temper. "To be fair, I shot your idea down, not you. But I'll give you credit for it if you want."

She rewarded him with a megawatt smile. "Deal. Now, show me what you've got in mind."

He described his evolving plans, leading her from one section to another while he illustrated with his hands.

"Fabulous," she approved enthusiastically. "Plus you've got a built-in market through Barrett's Mill Furniture. You play off their advertising and inventory. They get the kind of high-end custom pieces Chelsea's been dying to offer their customers. It's a win-win."

"Listen to you, sounding like some corporate bigwig. I think you've been hanging out with her too much."

"Or just enough. If I'm going to make a go of my art from here, I have to start thinking bigger. Set up a website so folks don't have to come here to buy my work. Things like that."

"Maybe we could go in on it together." Catching her hand, he reeled her into his arms where she belonged. "Y'know, share the costs and stuff."

"That depends," she said, tapping his chin. "What exactly were you thinking of sharing with me?"

He knew she was teasing him, but suddenly he wanted her to know exactly how he felt about her. Leaning in, he gave her a soft kiss. Then he gazed down into those incredible eyes and jumped.

"Everything, Jenna. I'm still not sure what you see in me, but whatever I've got you're welcome to it."

Meeting his tentative look with a confident one of her own, the smile she gave him warmed him right down to his toes. "Deal."

Chapter Eleven

Every year on Mother's Day, the Cross-roads Church hosted a gathering for all the moms, grandmothers, aunts and motherly women in town. It was open to anyone who wanted to bring a dish to pass and spend a couple of hours at a picnic with their neighbors.

Bruce Harkness had hauled his outdoor cookers across the street from The Whistlestop, and by the time Sunday service was over, the whole town smelled like his award-winning barbecue. Scott suspected that more than a few people who hadn't been planning to attend had been drawn in by that tantalizing aroma. With stars-and-stripes bunting already strung everywhere for the upcoming parade, the event reminded him of Memorial Day, minus the parade and fireworks.

"Wow, this is something else," Jenna commented as they wedged themselves onto a bench beside Amy and Jason. "Around here, there aren't usually this many folks all in one place unless there's a football game."

Scott stared at her in disbelief. "You like football?"

"As long as no one leaves in an ambulance. I know it's not ballroom dancing, but I hate to see any of those boys get hurt." He couldn't get over it, and she laughed. "Don't tell me—you played football in high school."

"All State wide receiver," Jason boasted, clapping him on the shoulder. "Scott caught most of Paul's touchdown passes their last year on the team together."

"Why am I not surprised to hear that?"

"We're Barretts," Scott reminded her with a grin. "It's what we do."

She rolled those gorgeous eyes at him, and he laughed. Not because of the conversation so much, but because it was a beautiful day, and he was surrounded by his kin, enjoying some of the best food in Virginia. They were jammed around two large picnic tables, and he did his best to keep up with several discussions flying around at once. Once everyone had filled their plates, Dad stood and waited for them to quiet down.

"I know you're all hungry, so I'll keep this short. I want to say, for the record—" he smiled at Mom, then circled the tables with a fond look "—that it's the women in this family who make it work. Day to day, year to year, you keep the rest of us on track and headed in the right direction. Without you, we'd all be lost."

"Because you wouldn't stop for directions," Mom added, blowing him an air kiss while she tapped her paper cup against his.

As if on cue, the women all laughed, while the Barrett men grudgingly admitted it was the truth.

"You can't help it," Jenna teased, nudging Scott's shoulder. "It's genetic."

"Yeah, I guess we can be pretty bull-headed."

Forking up some baked beans, she said, "Fortunately for you, I consider stubbornness to be a virtue."

"That's my girl," a feminine voice approved from behind them. "Tell it like it is."

Jenna's hand stopped midair, and very deliberately, she set her fork back down on her plate. When their guest stepped into view, Jenna's eyes darkened ominously, ended up somewhere near the color of thunderclouds.

Uh-oh, Scott thought with a wince. He'd done it now.

"What are you doing here?" she demanded

in a voice so lethally calm it sent chills up Scott's spine. "How did you even find me?"

"I think the phrase you're looking for is *Happy Mother's Day.*" A slightly older version of her daughter, Anastasia Reed had the same slender build and striking looks, with one major difference: she looked tired, as if life had started kicking her around at a young age and had worn her out long ago.

Sensing this wasn't going well, Scott got to his feet and offered his hand. "Ms. Reed, I'm Scott Barrett. It's nice to meet you."

"Same to you, handsome," she simpered, giving him a leisurely once-over that made him want to squirm. "Good-looking and determined. You've got a winner here, Jenna."

The anger on Jenna's face moments ago was nothing compared to the fury he saw there now. Clearly, he'd misjudged the comments she'd made during their romantic dinner, and tracking down her missing mother had been a horrible idea. Totally at a loss for what to do, he tried to stay calm and braced himself for a thorough dressing-down.

But it never came.

Without even glancing at him, Jenna climbed over the back of the bench and stalked away.

Standing there feeling like a moron, Scott tried to make light of the awkward situation. He figured his family didn't need to be in on this, so he angled Anastasia away from the tables filled with people obviously trying not to stare. "That went well."

"Actually, it did," she told him with a slight grin. "I was expecting her to slug me."

"Really?"

"Sure. If I was in her place, that's what I would have done." When he just gaped at her, she shrugged. "Hurt feelings can run awful deep, and that makes forgiveness come hard. Coming here, especially today, might have been a mistake on my part."

"But that's why I suggested Mother's Day," he protested, motioning back at the

Barrett clan. "She loves my mom and my gram. We all think of her as one of the family. I was hoping if you saw each other again, she'd finally have a chance to air out those bad feelings. Then you two could start mending fences and at least be friends."

"You seem like a sweet guy, but let me tell you something about my daughter. All her life, she did things her own way. Whether she got that from me or learned it from me, I'm not sure. I made the first move to make things better between us, and now it's up to her." Taking a business card from the pocket of her fitted leather jacket, she handed it to Scott. "The address is old, but my cell number hasn't changed. She can call me if she wants or not. It's her choice, but please tell her—" Tears welled in her expertly made-up eyes, and she paused to collect herself. "What I did might have been wrong, but it was the only way I knew to give her a better life than she ever could've had with me. I think about her every day, and I'm so proud of what she's accomplished."

He had no clue what to say, even less so when she reached into her oversize bag and pulled out a scrapbook. "Give this to her for me, would you? I might not see her again, and I want her to have it."

Scott wasn't keen on upsetting Jenna any more than he already had. "Can I look at it first?"

"Of course. It's not top secret or anything."

The way she said it reminded him of Jenna. Even though he'd clearly stepped over a line, he couldn't help feeling sad about Anastasia's missed opportunity to reconnect with her daughter.

"I'll make sure she gets it, then. Have a good trip back to Macon." She gave him a mournful smile, then turned and started walking toward a faded hatchback that had seen better days. As he watched her go, he thought about how much courage it must have taken for her to come here and wade into a sea of strangers, only to be cut down and sent away like some kind of criminal.

He called out her name, and she glanced over her shoulder. "Yes?"

"You've got a long drive ahead of you. Would you like to have something to eat before you go?"

Her eyes drifted over to the happy group, her wistful expression betraying just how much Jenna's rejection had stung. "I don't want to spoil your lunch."

"Not much chance of that. Besides, you came all this way, and it'd be a shame to send you home on an empty stomach."

"All right, then. If you're sure?"

"I'm sure."

Giving her an encouraging smile, he waited for her and they strolled back to the picnic together. While he made the introductions, his family quickly shifted from confused silence to welcoming her, and his mother slid down the bench to make room for their visitor. Scott mouthed a thank-you, and before long, the two mothers were chatting away like old friends.

It gave him time to catch his breath and finally have something to eat. Unfortunately, everything tasted like sawdust, and he laid his fork down with a sigh. Anastasia's comment about forgiveness coming hard rang in his head like a melancholy bell warning him about some impending doom.

By stepping into Jenna's very personal business, he realized he'd intruded somewhere he didn't belong. All he could do now was wait for her anger to recede enough so he could explain himself. And pray she could find a way to forgive him.

Just who did Scott Barrett think he was?

Seeing her white fingers, Jenna realized she had the steering wheel of her van in a death grip and relaxed her hold enough for the blood to start circulating again. She hadn't seen or heard from her mother in almost ten years and had done just fine on her own. Who was he to step into her private life in a clumsy attempt to reunite them? And today of all days, she railed silently, when people everywhere celebrated the women who loved them and made things better just by being there for them.

Women such as Diane and Olivia Barrett and, before long, Chelsea, who anyone could see was going to make a terrific mom. Caring and attentive, they were all capable of anchoring a family and guiding them through whatever came their way.

Not Anastasia Reed, though, Jenna thought grimly. Her visit hadn't been about reuniting with Jenna, but about easing her guilty conscience. Jenna could easily imagine the conversation between Scott and her mother, one cajoling, the other playing hard to get the way she always did with men. In the end, she'd allowed him to "convince" her he was right and had agreed to come to Barrett's Mill.

"Typical," she spat out, too angry to care that she was talking to herself. "The only person she's ever cared about is herself."

At her studio, she managed to stop herself short of slamming the driver's door like a four-year-old having a tantrum. Taking a few deep breaths, she stood with her keys in her hand, waiting for her temper to subside so she could think straight. As her thoughts began to make more sense, one rose to the surface with a clarity that was both frightening and sobering.

Scott had betrayed her.

Even in her current state, she recognized that his intentions had been admirable, but that didn't change the fact that he'd intruded somewhere he had absolutely no business going. Jenna had worked long and hard to get past being abandoned by the woman who should have been around to take care of her. In one misguided leap, Scott had managed to rip open those old wounds and bring back the pain she'd tried so desperately to escape.

Bad as that was, it was nothing compared to the pain of knowing she was the one who'd enabled him to do this to her. Against her better judgment, she'd allowed him to get close enough to hurt her. As much as it disgusted her to admit it, apparently she was her mother's daughter, after all.

Feeling defeated by her own stupidity, Jenna slunk into her darkened workroom and locked the door behind her. Tossing her keys and cell phone on a table, she crossed her arms and surveyed the tidy space, searching for something that might lift her spirits.

A glint of dark blue drew her attention to the chapel window hanging in its frame near the glass-front door. A sliver of sunlight had sneaked in around the drawn shade, finding its way to what she considered to be the most magnificent piece she'd ever had the privilege of working on. Strolling over to it, she couldn't help smiling as she admired the artist's vision and the skill it had taken to breathe life into such a fragile medium.

What had begun as a tribute to Will Barrett had become even more important to her because of Gretchen. Brought together by personal tragedy and their love of art, the two of them had formed a very special bond that meant as much to Jenna as any she'd ever experienced.

Except for one, she amended sadly, and blinked away a rare rush of tears. Optimistic by nature, she normally had little trouble keeping her less positive emotions in check. She confronted them, gave them a quick smack and moved on. Furious as she still was with Scott, she had a feeling it would take a lot more than that to get over him. Deeming him no longer trustworthy, her mind had already decided she'd be wise to leave him behind.

Her heart, however, was telling her a whole different story.

Arguing with herself was usually a pointless exercise in frustration, but she couldn't exactly ask someone else for advice. She'd painted herself into this corner, ignoring her better judgment to take a chance on someone who, until this morning, she'd considered worth the risk. What had really changed? she wondered as she sat down on a work table.

Her mother's unexpected—and unwelcome—reappearance had rocked her much more than she'd have thought possible until it happened. But why? Jenna was a grown woman now, and she had a good life despite the challenge of overcoming her mother's abandonment. While she pondered the root cause of her distress, gradually she realized she was going in circles and was no closer to an answer than she'd been when she'd started.

Sighing, she gave in to that helpless feeling and offered up a heartfelt prayer for guidance. She closed her eyes to blot out all the distractions around her and simply listened. After a few minutes, the answer filtered in, reminding her of the sunlight coming through the stained-glass window she and Gretchen had so painstakingly restored.

The real problem wasn't that her mother had resurfaced. It was that she'd come to Barrett's Mill, the one place Jenna valued enough to consider putting down roots and making a home. This was her place, and the last person she wanted to share it with was the woman who'd walked out on her and never looked back. Immature, maybe, but that was how she felt.

The question now was, what should she do about it?

While she was debating with herself, she heard a soft knock on the door. It didn't take a genius to know who was standing on the other side, and as nasty as it was, she was sorely tempted to ignore her visitor.

"Jenna, I know you're here," Scott began

in an apologetic drawl. "And I get why you don't wanna see me. Your mom left you something, and once you see it, I think you'll be glad to have it. I'm just gonna leave it out here and go."

After a few seconds, she heard his shoes crunching on the gravel in the driveway.

Don't let him go, a small but insistent voice in the back of her mind urged. It was her intuition, and any other time she would have followed it without reservation. This situation was different, though, and she hesitated.

Her internal tug-of-war resumed with a vengeance, but this time she recognized how futile her resistance was. Out front, Scott's pickup refused to start, and she glanced up with a little smile. "Okay, I get it. I'm going."

Unlocking the door, she went out and strolled over to the cranky sawmill truck. The wheezing starter finally conked out and did nothing but click when he turned the key. Groaning in exasperation, he banged his forehead on the steering wheel, and his shoulders heaved with a sigh so deep she almost could feel it herself.

Furious as she was with him, she didn't have the heart to let him suffer this way. He was just a man, after all. Relationships baffled the best of them.

Reaching through the open window, she rubbed his back in a comforting gesture. Since scolding him would only add to his misery, she opted for humor. "You really need to get yourself a new truck."

He swiveled his head to look out at her, his expression a treacherous mixture of sorrow and anger. "Ya think?"

"Don't snarl at me," she snapped, yanking her hand back the way she would with an unpredictable dog. "I'm just trying to help you."

"So, when you do it, it's okay, but when I do it, I'm the worst guy in the world?"

He had a point, but she wasn't in the mood

to be making concessions. With him seated in the truck, they were at eye level with each other, and she glared at him for all she was worth. "Those two scenarios are completely different, and you know it."

Something shifted in his eyes, and his stony expression gave way to a wry grin. "Yeah, but Mom said I was wrong and had to come tell you so."

"That sounds like her." She was still mad at him, but she couldn't help smiling. "Do you feel like a little kid again?"

"Pretty much. I'm so sorry for what I did," he added solemnly. "If I could go back and undo it, I would."

In those words, she heard more than an apology for what he'd done to her. It was a plea for forgiveness for the mistakes he'd made that had hurt the people he cared most about, and who cared about him. He'd come a long way, but he still had some work to do. Viewed from that perspective, his efforts to bring Mom and her back together—misguided as they were—struck her as incredibly sweet.

"I understand why you did it." His demeanor brightened, and she shook a stern finger at him. "But I'm still furious with you, so don't think you're off the hook or anything. The last person I wanted to see today was my weak, self-centered mother."

"You know that's ironic, right? I mean, it's Mother's Day."

"Don't get smart with me, Barrett. You're on very thin ice here." Her blustering didn't make much of a dent with him, and she couldn't help responding to the crooked grin he was wearing. "You're hopeless."

"Actually, that's one of the nicest things a woman's ever said about me."

As he climbed from the cab, she snorted derisively. "Why do I have no trouble believing that?"

He made no move to touch her, but as the gaze they shared grew less combative, she felt as if he had. The strength he carried with him wrapped around her as surely as any embrace, drawing her closer the way it had the very first day she met him.

"I'd never intentionally do anything to hurt you," he murmured, dark eyes glimmering with the fondness she'd seen in them more often lately. Suddenly, the emotion in them deepened, and alarm bells began clanging in her head. He wasn't holding her, and she could easily retreat from him. But as hard as she tried, she simply couldn't make herself look away.

"I love you, Jenna."

Her heart thudded to a stop, and she vigorously shook her head to dispel the terrifying thought. "No, you don't."

"Yeah, I do. Trust me, I'm not crazy about it, either," he confided with a sigh. "I've got enough going on without adding you to the mix."

"How flattering."

Groaning, he looked at his shoes and shook his head before focusing back on her. "Sorry, I'm not doing this right. What I meant was, I wasn't planning on falling in love with you. It happened when I wasn't paying attention. Does that make any sense at all?"

Jenna wasn't sure what to say to that, and while she searched for an appropriate response, she mulled over his stunning revelation.

Scott Barrett was in love with her.

She knew how intimidating it was to go out on that limb and be the first to say it with no guarantee you'd hear it in return. Determined not to follow her mother's deplorable example with men, Jenna had never offered those priceless words to any man she'd known, even when they'd begged her to.

But this was different. Scott wasn't pleading for her affection, because he already had it. Abruptly, it dawned on her that somewhere along the way she'd fallen in love with him, too.

Closing the gap he'd left between them, she dangled her arms over those broad shoulders and put an end to his obvious misery. "I guess it make sense, because that's what happened to me."

"You mean—"

She cut him off with a long, delicious kiss. Pulling back, she smiled up at the one man she'd ever known who loved her enough and was stubborn enough to refuse to let her walk away from him. "I love you, too."

Joy flooded his eyes, and he nearly crushed her in a grateful hug.

"I'm still mad at you," she warned, cozily circled in his arms. "You went way out of bounds, tracking down my mother like that. How did you manage it, anyway?"

"I knew her name and where you were living ten years ago. With the internet, it really wasn't that hard. To be honest, I'm a little puzzled why you didn't try it yourself."

It was impossible to properly explain her motives to someone who didn't understand how it felt to be tossed aside like trash. For lack of anything better, she said, "She left me behind, and I never wanted to see her again."

"You might feel differently when you see what she brought for you."

Jenna's eyes drifted to the book he'd left beside her front door. After all these years, the little girl who still existed inside her hopped up excitedly, wondering about her gift. Wary of being disappointed yet again, the adult side of her marched in and took over. "Maybe."

"I can stay, if you want." Seeming to sense her conflicting emotions, Scott gave her shoulders an encouraging squeeze. "Come on. It's just a book. It can't hurt you."

It could flatten her, though, and she wasn't up for that right now. Then again, if he was with her, she'd be able to handle it better. Oddly enough, she didn't consider tucking the book away and never opening it.

Foolish or curious? she asked herself.

Probably a bit of both. "Okay, let's get this over with."

Taking a deep breath, she opened the scrapbook and on the first page in scripted letters she saw her name arched over her very first drawing: a faded sketch of a kitten she'd scribbled on a Dairy Queen napkin. In the bottom corner was the date, added in her mother's handwriting. Running a fingertip over it, Jenna whispered, "I did this when I was four. I can't believe she kept it all this time."

Scott didn't say anything, but he edged closer and put an arm around her. She needed every ounce of his comforting presence as she leafed through the artistic retrospective of her life from elementary-school art-show awards to recent newspaper articles applauding her unique creative style. By the time she got to the final page, the tears she'd been holding back were too much for her.

Suddenly exhausted, she buried her face

in Scott's chest and gave in to years' worth of bitterness and frustration. She cried for the girl she had been, and the rootless young woman who'd roamed the country searching for a place she could finally call home.

When she'd calmed down a bit, she let out a heavy sigh. "All this time I thought she didn't care where I was or what I was doing. But she did."

"I got to talk to her at the picnic," he said, kissing the top of Jenna's head. "She said she left to give you a chance at a better life. I got the feeling she believed she wasn't enough family for you."

"But she could've been." Jenna sobbed as more tears rushed in. "All she had to do was try."

"Maybe she didn't know how," he reasoned in a gentle tone. "Or she saw how much you liked Vicky's family and thought you'd be happier with them."

Jenna angled her head back and met his

sympathetic gaze. "Your mom would never have done that to you."

"No, but she wasn't on her own, either. Her parents used to live in Cambridge, and she's got family all over the area who would've helped her if she needed it. You guys moved around a lot, so your mom had to handle everything by herself."

"Having a new boyfriend every month didn't help much, either."

"I'm not touching that one."

"Smart man." When his comments registered with her more clearly, she asked, "Did she really tell you she left so I'd have a real family?"

"That was my take on it, anyway. If you wanna know for sure what she meant, you'll have to ask her yourself."

Direct and to the point, the response was typical Scott. While he'd stopped short of telling her what to do, he hadn't skirted the issue, either. He'd given her his opinion, and the rest was up to her. "I'll think about it."

"Good for you."

Because she wasn't ready to let him go just yet, Jenna cuddled against him, savoring the sensation of feeling safe and protected. She didn't know if she had it in her to forgive her mother's behavior, but she made herself a promise.

She wouldn't allow the shadows in her past to keep her from making a bright future with this wonderful, complicated man. She loved Scott, and he loved her. For her, that was more than enough.

Chapter Twelve

"Wow," Scott breathed, standing back to admire the restored stained-glass window. "It looks incredible."

"It really does, doesn't it? Once I had the glass cutting and snapping technique down, Jenna let me do most of the work," Gretchen added, glancing up at her father for his reaction.

"Hard to believe you could piece it all back together," he agreed, giving her a proud hug around the shoulders. Over her head, he met Jenna's eyes and mouthed, *Bless you*.

"She's a natural," Jenna told him, winking

at her eager assistant. "Any time you want some extra money, there's always plenty for you to do at my studio."

"Maybe I could even do my own projects someday," she suggested, enthusiasm lighting her eyes.

"A definite possibility." Jenna's cell phone rang, and she pulled it from the bib pocket on her overalls. "It's my stained-glass guru, Kurt. I can get back to him later."

"We've gotta be going anyway," Gretchen said with a sigh. "My chem final is tomorrow, and I've got some last-minute cramming to do."

"Attagirl. School first." Jenna held up her hand for a high five. "Knock 'em dead, kiddo."

"I will. And thanks again for letting us help you guys put the window in. It's really cool seeing it back where it belongs."

"It sure is," Scott agreed as he and Jenna walked their guests to their car. "Have a good one."

After the Lewises had driven away, the text alert on Jenna's phone went off, and then she saw the voice-mail notification pop up, as well. "It's Kurt. Must be important."

Curious, she put the phone on speaker and hit the button for her voice mail. Without preamble, his voice came over the tiny speakers, shouting above the din of a grinding wheel in the background.

"Have I got a proposition for you. A buddy of mine is starting up a gallery in Knoxville, and one of his artists just backed out of the opening. I showed him that portfolio you put online, and he's very interested in seeing some of your current work. The only hitch is he wants the artists on-site to meet buyers, maybe take on some custom orders to help get the business up and running. I know you're dug in for the summer, but Tennessee's not all that far to drive to meet him. Let me know what happens."

"He sounds pretty excited," Scott commented with a chuckle. "You'd think it was him getting the interview."

"That's Kurt," she explained with a fond smile. "I think I remind him of his daughter."

"She's an artist, too?" Scott asked as they settled into the chairs on the front porch.

"Marine biologist. But she's passionate about what she does, and he's really proud of her. She lives on her boat, and he replaced the original windows with a series of stained-glass ocean scenes. They're gorgeous."

The text he'd sent her included a connection to the gallery's website. She recognized Milo Polhein's name from her years on the circuit, and smiled when she read in the bio section that marriage and impending fatherhood had convinced him it was time to settle down somewhere. Being a native Tennessean, he'd chosen his hometown and was now actively acquiring distinctive pieces for discerning clients seeking only the very best.

Translation: people with excellent taste and the money to back it up. Any artist she'd ever met would have jumped at this opportunity, she knew. Her mind wandered back to her conversation with Chelsea and Amy in the nursery when she'd confided to them that seeing her work hanging in a high-end gallery would be a dream come true.

She left the gallery's home page up on her screen and stared at it, trying to sort through the thoughts flying around in her head.

"What're you thinking?" Scott asked.

When she looked over, she saw him leaning back in his chair, a beat-up work boot across one knee in the careless pose that probably fooled a lot of people. Not her, though. She'd learned to check his eyes if she really wanted to know how he felt about something. In them, she found a blend of curiosity and fear, as if he was anxious to hear her answer and dreading it at the same time.

"I'm not sure. I mean, a couple months ago I would've pounced on something like this. But now..." She shrugged.

"You're not saying that 'cause of me, are you?"

Balancing her elbows on the arm of her chair closest to his, she smiled. "You mean, because you said you love me?"

"You said you love me, too," he pointed out with a cocky grin. "Remember?"

The lighter tone made her laugh. "How could I forget? It was only yesterday."

"Best day of my life."

The deft shift to a more serious attitude nearly gave her whiplash, and she pivoted to keep up. Leaning in, she gave him a leisurely kiss that made them both smile.

"Mine, too. Things are going really well for us, and that means everything to me. But this is an incredible break for me, so now I'm torn. I've been working toward something like this for a long time, but I don't wanna mess up what we have."

"Giving up on your dream would do that, big-time," he informed her sternly. "I don't want you looking back in a few years, wondering what you could've accomplished if you'd just taken that leap. Go talk to this Milo guy. See what he has to say. After that, you'll know what to do."

Scott was showing the utmost faith in her, and Jenna recognized just how far he'd come from the cynical man who'd first crossed her path all those weeks ago. Not only had he readjusted to life in his hometown, he'd learned to trust people again. The transformation was too stunning for words, and she knew God had more than a slight hand in it.

"Well, I suppose it wouldn't hurt to go to Knoxville and meet him." Inspiration struck, and she sat up excitedly. "Is there any way you can come with me?"

Grimacing, he shook his head. "Even if the law would let me, I wouldn't go along.

This is your thing, Jenna. You don't need me tagging after you, making it all more complicated than it needs to be."

"I don't feel that way."

"I appreciate that, but I'm staying here, out of your way." Brushing a kiss over her lips, he murmured, "Don't worry. I'll be here when you get home."

Home.

That simple word hit her hard, because that was how she felt when she was with him: at home. It hadn't escaped her that he'd painted his house her favorite color and had let her plant whatever kind of flowers she wanted in the neglected garden. They could make this their place, she knew, and the pull of that new dream was almost more than she could resist.

But he wouldn't allow her to settle down in Barrett's Mill until she was absolutely certain she didn't want something else. More than anything, it told her just how much he loved her. Wanting her there with him, but willing to let her go, because her happiness was as important to him as his own.

"You better be here," she retorted, hoping to buoy his drooping spirits. "Because I love you, you crazy, obstinate man, and I'll be back."

The three days Jenna was gone felt more like a month.

Scott had grown accustomed to spending most of his off-hours with her, and without her lively company to distract and entertain him, time pretty much stood still. He envisioned her schmoozing with the gallery owner and other artists, enjoying some time with people as creative as she was. It must be fun for her to share stories and discuss concepts with folks who actually understood what she was talking about. A far cry from being the only artist in a town buried in the shadows of the Blue Ridge Mountains. He knew it was pointless to wonder what she was thinking, but at times he simply couldn't help himself.

Those were the times when he forced himself to focus on something—anything—besides what might be going on in Knoxville. The good news was he'd finished Amy's headboard way ahead of schedule, and his sister-in-law was thrilled.

The bad news was he'd come up with several different scenarios for Jenna's homecoming, and most of them ended badly. Worst-case scenario, he figured she'd be offered the spot in Milo's opening and snap it up because it was her dream. Then she'd get attached to the more exciting pace of life in Knoxville and never come back. Best-case scenario, she'd get the offer, decide it wasn't the right fit for her free-spirited soul and turn it down. Then she'd settle permanently in Barrett's Mill. With him.

In his saner moments, he recognized that the second option was about as selfish as it could get, and he chided himself for thinking that way. This was Jenna's career, after all, and her life. While their growing feelings for one another might end up playing a role in her decision, they shouldn't be front and center. In his experience, the middle alternative normally won out, and he resigned himself to the likelihood that she'd eventually decide to take the temporary spot in Milo's gallery.

The notion that it might not be offered to her never occurred to him. While he wasn't an expert, he could see her work had a special quality to it. Whether humorous garden gnome or touching family portrait, everything she created possessed some kind of emotion that spoke to people. Even to him, someone who'd always leaned more toward the practical end of the spectrum than the sentimental. Jenna had helped him find something in himself he hadn't known was there before he met her. Now that it was out in the open, he had to find a way to deal with it.

The trouble was he couldn't tackle this dilemma with his usual pragmatic mindset. Strong feelings such as these couldn't be reasoned away. He searched for another approach but came up blank.

Personal tug-of-war wasn't his favorite pastime, so Scott paused in his sweeping of the chapel floor to glance up for a quick request. "Whatever she ends up doing, I just want to be able take it well. If You could help me make that happen, I'd really appreciate it."

He felt a slight pressure on his shoulder, as if someone had reached down to give him an encouraging pat. It reminded him of the way Granddad had reassured him as a boy, and the memory made him smile. With Jenna's unwavering support, he'd finally forgiven himself for missing his grandfather's last days and had fully embraced the legacy he'd received.

He never would have chosen to gain his first home this way, but now he viewed his inheritance as the blessing it was. If only circumstances would allow him to share it with Jenna, he'd be a happy man.

When he finished cleaning, he took inventory of his supplies and made a list for his next visit to Stegall's Hardware. Now that he'd made peace with his past, he preferred to do business in person rather than dodging contact with the residents of his hometown. Even folks who'd started out with frosty stares had begun to come around, and he was pleased to discover his persistence was beginning to pay off. Just as Jenna had predicted, he thought with a grin.

As if on cue, through a side window he saw her van coming up the driveway. Reminding himself to let her do the talking, he set his list on a table and forced himself to walk slowly. He didn't want her to think he was some pathetic puppy dog who'd been counting the hours until she came back. Even if that was how he'd been feeling.

She parked next to his truck, and he

strolled over to kiss her through the open driver's window. "Hey there."

"Hey yourself." Bathing him in one of her amazing smiles, she leaned her arms on the frame. "Whatcha doin'?"

"Waiting for you." The response flew from his mouth all on its own, and he followed it with an embarrassed groan. "Sorry about that."

"Sorry?" She climbed out to stand in front of him. Giving him one of those knowing feminine looks, she stepped closer and snaked her arms around his waist. "For missing me or for admitting it?"

He must have been losing his grip, because it never occurred to him to go the macho route and claim he was just kidding. "Neither, actually. Is that bad?"

She rewarded him with a long kiss that made those three miserable days vanish in a heartbeat. Looping his arms around her, he braced himself for whatever came next. "So, how'd things go in Knoxville?"

"Great. Milo's a hoot, and his gallery is in a trendy neighborhood surrounded by other artists, writers and performers. Most of them live there, and they attract a lot of young people and families. It's a fabulous place, and yesterday he offered me a spot in the opening."

Scott's heart hit the ground with a thud, and he struggled to keep his expression from diving down after it. "Sounds like a perfect fit for you."

"It would be," she agreed, fingering the collar on his shirt. "Except for one thing."

"What's that?"

"You're here with your own business to launch. I'm pretty good at thinking outside the box, but I still haven't come up with a way to be in two places at once."

His foolish heart rebounded like a rubber ball, and he did his best to catch it before he got emotional whiplash. "What're you saying?"

He wanted to hear the words. No, he

realized, it was more than that. He needed to hear this beautiful, aggravating woman tell him she was choosing him over the professional opportunity she'd dreamed of for so many years.

The coy smile she gave him told him she'd picked up on his unspoken wish. "That I'd rather be here with you."

"Are you sure? I mean, this gallery slot could be a once-in-a-lifetime kinda thing."

"So are you."

A flood of emotions was threatening to swamp him, and he drew her in for a long, grateful kiss. "Love you."

"I love you, too." Eyes sparkling in fun, she added, "The hermit and the artist. Who'd have thunk it, huh?"

Chuckling, he flipped her single braid back over her shoulder. "Not me, that's for sure."

These days, though, he couldn't seem to think about much else. So, before he could lose his nerve, he plunged ahead. "I had a lot of time to mull things over while you were gone, and I've been wanting to ask you something."

"Shoot."

He'd run a dozen different speeches through his mind, but every one of them evaporated when he looked into those sparkling blue eyes.

"Jenna, my life got better the day I met you. You're patient with me, but you don't let me get by with any nonsense, either. It may not always seem like it, but I'm grateful for everything you've done to help me, and I love you more than you'll ever know. Will you marry me?"

"Yes," she breathed without hesitation, wrapping him in the kind of warm embrace he knew he'd never get tired of if he lived a hundred years. "There's one condition, though."

She held up her pointer finger, and he grasped that talented hand and held it against his chest. "Anything you want."

"We have to get married here, in the chapel. It means a lot to your family, and restoring it is what brought us together. We should make it part of our wedding day."

Coming from her, the request made perfect sense, and he smiled. "Works for me."

Epilogue

"I haven't been out here in years," Olivia said, looking around the old homestead with a fond expression. Coming back to Scott and Jenna, she beamed at them. "It looks like a home again. Will would be so proud of what you two have done with this place."

Jenna had spent most of the summer wrestling the yard into shape while Scott rehabbed what was now a cheerful yellow cottage set in the woods. It had been a lot of hard work, but also a labor of love they'd both dedicated to the generous man who'd found a way to nudge his wayward grandson back onto a better path.

And now, on a crisp September day, their wedding guests were milling around the chapel, admiring the fine woodwork and, of course, the stunning window.

With a smile for her husband, Jenna asked Olivia, "Did Scott tell you our plans for the chapel?"

"No." Edging closer, she whispered, "Is it a secret?"

"Not anymore," Scott joked with a grin. "We're gonna combine our two businesses and run them from here. We're still working on a name, but since we're both Barretts now, that should make it easier to come up with something."

"You'll stay at the mill, though, won't you?"

"Yeah. With the busy season coming up, Paul needs me."

Jenna heard the pride in his voice and barely managed to keep from hugging him.

He'd come so far this year, she sometimes had trouble believing he was the same cool, distant man she'd met at Will's grave site that spring.

When she noticed one of their guests looking slightly out of place, she called out, "Tess!"

The slender young woman she'd met in California last year glanced at Jenna, and a grateful smile replaced her apprehensive expression. They'd invited her, hoping Tess would take the opportunity to get acquainted with her extended family in Virginia. Still, Jenna couldn't begin to imagine how much courage it took to travel across the country to meet dozens of strangers at a wedding. Then again, being a Barrett, Tess clearly had plenty of attitude to spare.

Joining them, she handed Scott an envelope. "A little something from me to help you two get your studio up and running."

No mention of her parents, Jenna noted with curiosity. Interesting.

Scott thanked her with a smile, and Olivia slipped an arm around her in a quick hug. "Are you having fun getting to know everyone?"

"Definitely. I just wish I could keep them all straight."

"If you come back and stay awhile, that will help," her grandmother suggested in her usual, non-subtle fashion. "There's a room in my house for you whenever you want it."

"Thanks, Gram. I just might take you up on that."

"I'm going to go help Diane in the kitchen, and we can use an extra pair of hands. Why don't you come with me?" Standing on tiptoe, Olivia kissed Scott's cheek, then Jenna's. "You've made this a wonderful day for our entire family. God bless you both."

As Jenna watched them go, a sudden rush of emotion caught in her throat. "Olivia's an amazing woman, isn't she?"

"All the Barrett women are." Embracing her from behind, he dropped a kiss on her shoulder. "Which reminds me, what'd your mom have to say when she called this morning?"

"That she'd come for a visit soon. She appreciated the invitation, but she said she didn't want to make things tense for us on our special day." Sighing, Jenna went on. "We have a ways to go still, and we may never be as close as we could've been, but I think we can make it work."

"You're welcome."

Spinning in his embrace, she did her best to glare at him. But really, it was their wedding day, and she didn't have the heart to be truly angry with the only man she'd ever come across who saw all her quirks and loved her in spite of them. Judging by his shameless grin, the gesture had no impact on him anyway. "Did I say thank you?"

"Not yet, but you will." Circling his arms around her, he gave her a light kiss. "I'm spending the rest of my life with you, so I can wait."

Unable to resist the unique combination of arrogance and tenderness that made Scott who he was, she cuddled against him with a contented sigh.

This definitely worked for her.

* * * * *

Dear Reader,

As the title suggests, this is a story about finding your way home. Wrapped up tightly with that is having faith—in God, in the people around us, but mostly in ourselves.

It's the thing Scott needs most since being released from prison. His reluctance to trust anyone outside his own family leaves him feeling lonely and isolated. While his hometown should have felt welcoming, for Scott it's not that simple. Some people accept him, and some view him with suspicion. Fortunately, Jenna makes up her own mind about folks, and despite his checkered history, she sees plenty of good in him. Her lightheartedness draws him out of that dark past and toward a promising future—with her.

I'm a firm believer in second chances. We might go astray, but with some solid, honest work, we can get ourselves back on the right path. As Scott learns, the first step is to shut out all the everyday noise and listen to what God is trying to tell us. Following that voice is seldom easy, but it leads us to where we're meant to be.

If you'd like to stop by for a visit, you'll find me online at miaross.com, Facebook, Twitter and Goodreads. While you're there, send me a message in your favorite format. I'd love to hear from you!

Mia Ross

REQUEST YOUR FREE BOOKS!

2 FREE RIVETING INSPIRATIONAL NOVELS IN TRUE LARGE PRINT PLUS 2 FREE MYSTERY GIFTS

TRUE LARGE PRINT

YES! Please send me 2 FREE Love Inspired® Suspense True Large Print novels and my 2 FREE mystery gifts (gifts are worth about $10). After receiving them, if I don't wish to receive any more books, I can return the shipping statement marked "cancel." If I don't cancel, I will receive 3 brand-new true large print novels every month and be billed just $7.99 per book in the U.S. or $9.99 per book in Canada. That's a savings of at least 20% off the cover price. It's quite a bargain! Shipping and handling is just 50¢ per book in the U.S. and 75¢ per book in Canada.* I understand that accepting the 2 free books and gifts places me under no obligation to buy anything. I can always return the shipment and cancel at any time. Even if I never buy another book, the two free books and gifts are mine to keep forever.

124/324 IDN F5GD

Name   (PLEASE PRINT)

Address   Apt. #

City   State/Prov.   Zip/Postal Code

Signature (if under 18, a parent or guardian must sign)

Mail to the Harlequin® Reader Service:
IN U.S.A.: P.O. Box 1867, Buffalo, NY 14240-1867
IN CANADA: P.O. Box 609, Fort Erie, Ontario L2A 5X3

* Terms and prices subject to change without notice. Prices do not include applicable taxes. Sales tax applicable in N.Y. Canadian residents will be charged applicable taxes. Offer not valid in Quebec. This offer is limited to one order per household. Not valid for current subscribers to Love Inspired Suspense True Large Print books. All orders subject to credit approval. Credit or debit balances in a customer's account(s) may be offset by any other outstanding balance owed by or to the customer. Please allow 4 to 6 weeks for delivery. Offer available while quantities last.

Your Privacy—The Harlequin® Reader Service is committed to protecting your privacy. Our Privacy Policy is available online at www.ReaderService.com or upon request from the Harlequin Reader Service.

We make a portion of our mailing list available to reputable third parties that offer products we believe may interest you. If you prefer that we not exchange your name with third parties, or if you wish to clarify or modify your communication preferences, please visit us at www.ReaderService.com/consumerchoice or write to us at Harlequin Reader Service Preference Service, P.O. Box 9062, Buffalo, NY 14269. Include your complete name and address.

Reader Service.com

Manage your account online!

- Review your order history
- Manage your payments
- Update your address

---

*We've designed
the Harlequin® Reader Service
website just for you.*

Enjoy all the features!

- Reader excerpts from any series
- Respond to mailings and
  special monthly offers
- Discover new series available to you
- Browse the Bonus Bucks catalogue
- Share your feedback

Visit us at:
ReaderService.com